Great Detective Stories

A WATERMILL CLASSIC

Contents of this edition copyright © 1986 by Watermill Press

Printed in the United States of America.

ISBN 0-8167-0800-2

10 9 8 7 6 5 4 3

Contents

Arthur Conan Doyle

The Boscombe Valley Mystery

We were seated at breakfast one morning, my wife and I, when the maid brought in a telegram. It was from Sherlock Holmes and ran in this way:

> Have you a couple of days to spare? Have just been wired for from the west of England in connection with Boscombe Valley tragedy. Shall be glad if you will come with me. Air and scenery perfect. Leave Paddington by the 11:15.

"What do you say, dear?" said my wife, looking across at me. "Will you go?"

"I really don't know what to say. I have a fairly long list at present."

"Oh, Anstruther would do your work for you. You have been looking a little pale lately. I think that the change would do you good, and you are always so interested in Mr. Sherlock Holmes's cases."

"I should be ungrateful if I were not, seeing what I gained through one of them," I answered. "But if I am to go, I must pack at once, for I have only half an hour."

My experience of camp life in Afghanistan had at least had the effect of making me a prompt and ready traveler. My wants were few and simple, so that in less than the time stated I was in a cab with my valise, rattling away to Paddington Station. Sherlock Holmes was pacing up and down the platform, his tall, gaunt figure made even gaunter and taller by his long gray traveling cloak and close-fitting cloth cap.

"It is really very good of you to come, Watson," said he. "It makes a considerable difference to me, having someone with me on whom I can thoroughly rely. Local aid is always either worthless or else biased. If you will keep the two corner seats I shall get the tickets."

We had the carriage to ourselves save for an immense litter of papers which Holmes had brought with him. Among these he rummaged and read, with intervals of note-taking and of meditation, until we were past Reading. Then he suddenly rolled them all into a gigantic ball and tossed them up onto the rack.

"Have you heard anything of the case?" he asked.

"Not a word. I have not seen a paper for some days."

"The London press has not had very full accounts. I have just been looking through all the recent papers in order to master the particulars. It seems, from what I gather, to be one of those simple cases which are so extremely difficult."

"That sounds a little paradoxical."

"But it is profoundly true. Singularity is almost invariably a clue. The more featureless and commonplace a crime is, the more difficult it is to bring it home. In this case, however, they have established a very serious case against the son of the murdered man."

"It is a murder, then?"

"Well, it is conjectured to be so. I shall take nothing for granted until I have the opportunity of looking personally into it. I will explain the state of things to you, as far as I have been able to understand it, in a very few words.

"Boscombe Valley is a country district not very far from Ross, in Herefordshire. The largest landed proprietor in that part is a Mr. John Turner, who made his money in Australia and returned some years ago to the old country. One of the farms which he held, that of Hatherley, was let to Mr. Charles McCarthy, who was also an ex-Australian. The men had known each other in the colonies, so that it was not unnatural that when they came to settle down they should do so as near each other as possible. Turner was apparently the richer man, so McCarthy became his tenant but still remained, it seems, upon terms of perfect equality, as they were frequently together. McCarthy had one son, a lad of eighteen, and Turner had an only daughter of the same age, but neither of them had wives living. They appear to have avoided the society of the neighboring English families and to have led retired lives, though both the McCarthys were fond of sport and were frequently seen at the race meetings of the neighborhood. McCarthy kept two servants—a man and a girl. Turner had a considerable household, some half-dozen at the least. That is as much as I have been able to gather about the families. Now for the facts.

"On June 3rd, that is, on Monday last, McCarthy left his house at Hatherley about three in the afternoon and walked down to the Boscombe Pool, which is a small lake formed by the spreading out of the stream which runs down the Boscombe Valley. He had been out with his serving man in the morning at Ross, and he had told the man that he must hurry, as he had an appointment of importance to keep at three. From that appointment he never came back alive.

"From Hatherley Farmhouse to the Boscombe Pool is a quarter of a mile, and two people saw him as he passed over this ground. One was an old woman, whose name is not mentioned, and the other was William Crowder, a gamekeeper in the employ of Mr. Turner. Both these witnesses depose that Mr. McCarthy was walking alone. The gamekeeper adds that within a few minutes of his seeing Mr. McCarthy pass, he had seen his son, Mr. James McCarthy, going the same way with a gun under his arm. To the best of his belief, the father was actually in sight at the time, and the son was following him. He thought no more of the matter until he heard in the evening of the tragedy that had occurred.

"The two McCarthy's were seen after the time when William Crowder, the gamekeeper, lost sight of them. The Boscombe Pool is thickly wooded round, with just a fringe of grass and of reeds round the edge. A girl of fourteen, Patience Moran, who is the daughter of the lodgekeeper of the Boscombe Valley estate, was in one of the woods picking flowers. She states that while she was there she saw, at the border of the wood and close by the lake, Mr. McCarthy and his son, and that they appeared to be having a violent quarrel. She heard Mr. McCarthy the elder using very strong language to his son, and she saw the latter raise up his hand as if to strike his father. She was so frightened by their violence that she ran away and told her mother when she reached home that she had left the two McCarthys quarreling near Boscombe Pool, and that she was afraid that they were going to fight. She had hardly said the words when young McCarthy came running up to the lodge to say he had found his father dead in the wood, and to ask for the help of the lodgekeeper. He was much excited, without either his gun or his hat, and his right hand and sleeve were observed to be stained with fresh blood. On following him they found the dead body stretched out upon the grass beside the pool. The head had been beaten in by repeated blows of some heavy and blunt weapon. The injuries were such as might very well have been inflicted by the butt-end of his son's gun, which was found lying on the grass within a few paces of the body. Under these circumstances the young man was instantly arrested, and a verdict of "willful murder" having been returned at the inquest on Tuesday, he was on Wednesday brought before the magistrates at Ross, who have referred the case to the next Assizes. Those are the main facts of the case as they came out before the coroner and the police court.''

''I could hardly imagine a more damning case,'' I remarked. ''If ever circumstantial evidence pointed to a criminal it does so here.''

''Circumstantial evidence is a very tricky thing,'' answered Holmes thoughtfully. ''It may seem to point very straight to one thing, but if you shift your own point of view a little, you may find it pointing in an equally uncompromising manner to something entirely different. It must be confessed, however, that the case looks exceedingly grave against the young man, and it is very possible that he is indeed the culprit. There are several people in the neighborhood, however, and among them Miss Turner, the daughter of the neighboring landowner, who believe in his innocence, and who have retained Lestrade, whom you may recollect in connection with 'A Study in Scarlet,' to work out the case in his interest. Lestrade, being rather puzzled, has referred the case to me, and hence it is that two middle-aged gentlemen are flying westward at fifty miles an hour instead of quietly digesting their breakfasts at home.''

''I am afraid,'' said I, ''that the facts are so obvious that you will find little credit to be gained out of this case.''

''There is nothing more deceptive than an obvious fact,'' he answered, laughing. ''Besides, we may chance to hit upon some other obvious facts which may have been by no means obvious to Mr. Lestrade. You know me too well to think that I am boasting when I say that I shall either confirm or destroy his theory by means which he is quite incapable of employing, or even of understanding. To take the first example to hand, I very clearly perceive that in your bedroom the window is upon the right-hand side, and yet I question whether Mr. Lestrade would have noted even so self-evident a thing as that.''

''How on earth—''

''My dear fellow, I know you well. I know the military neatness which characterizes you. You shave every morning, and in this season you shave by the sunlight; but since your shaving is less and less complete as we get farther back on the left side, until it becomes positively slovenly as we get round the angle of the jaw, it is surely very clear that that side is less illuminated than the other. I could not imagine a man of your habits looking at himself in an equal light and being satisfied with such a result. I only quote this as a trivial example of observation and inference. Therein lies my *métier*, and it is just possible that it may be of some service in the investigation which lies before us. There are one or two minor points which were brought out in the inquest, and which are worth considering.''

''What are they?''

''It appears that his arrest did not take place at once, but after the return to Hatherley Farm. On the inspector of constabulary informing him that he was a prisoner, he remarked that he was not surprised to hear it, and that it was no more than his deserts. This observation of his had the natural effect of removing any traces of doubt which might have remained in the minds of the coroner's jury.''

7

"It was a confession," I ejaculated.

"No, for it was followed by a protestation of innocence."

"Coming on the top of such a damning series of events, it was at least a most suspicious remark."

"On the contrary," said Holmes, "it is the brightest rift which I can at present see in the clouds. However innocent he might be, he could not be such an absolute imbecile as not to see that the circumstances were very black against him. Had he appeared surprised at his own arrest, or feigned indignation at it, I should have looked upon it as highly suspicious, because such surprise or anger would not be natural under the circumstances, and yet might appear to be the best policy to a scheming man. His frank acceptance of the situation marks him as either an innocent man, or else as a man of considerable self-restraint and firmness. As to his remark about his deserts, it was also not unnatural if you consider that he stood beside the dead body of his father, and that there is no doubt that he had that very day so far forgotten his filial duty as to bandy words with him, and even, according to the little girl whose evidence is so important, to raise his hand as if to strike him. The self-reproach and contrition which are displayed in his remark appear to me to be the signs of a healthy mind rather than of a guilty one."

I shook my head. "Many men have been hanged on far slighter evidence," I remarked.

"So they have. And many men have been wrongfully hanged."

"What is the young man's own account of the matter?"

"It is, I am afraid, not very encouraging to his supporters, though there are one or two points in it which are suggestive. You will find it here, and may read it for yourself."

He picked out from his bundle a copy of the local Herefordshire paper, and having turned down the sheet he pointed out the paragraph in which the unfortunate young man had given his own statement of what had occurred. I settled myself down in the corner of the carriage and read it very carefully. It ran in this way:

Mr. James McCarthy, the only son of the deceased, was then called and gave evidence as follows: "I had been away from home for three days at Bristol, and had only just returned upon the morning of last Monday, the 3rd. My father was absent from home at the time of my arrival, and I was informed by the maid that he had driven over to Ross with John Cobb, the groom. Shortly after my return I heard the wheels of his trap in the yard, and, looking out of my window, I saw him get out and walk rapidly out of the yard, though I was not aware in which direction he was going. I then took my gun and strolled out in the direction of the Boscombe Pool, with the intention of visiting the rabbit warren which is upon the other side. On my way I saw William Crowder, the gamekeeper, as he had stated in his evidence; but he is mistaken in thinking that I was following my father. I had no idea that he was in front of me. When about a hundred yards from the pool I heard a cry of 'Cooee!' which was a usual signal between my father and myself. I then hurried forward, and found him standing by the pool. He appeared to be much surprised at seeing me and asked me rather roughly what I was doing there. A conversation ensued which led to high violent temper. Seeing that his passion was becoming ungovernable, I left him and returned towards Hatherley Farm. I had not gone more than 150 yards, however, when I heard a hideous outcry behind me, which caused me to run back again. I found my father expiring upon the ground, with his head terribly injured. I dropped my gun and held him in my arms, but he almost instantly expired. I knelt beside him for some minutes, and then made my way to Mr. Turner's lodgekeeper, his house being the nearest, to ask for assistance. I saw no one near my father when I returned, and I have no idea how he came by his injuries. He was not a popular man, being somewhat cold and forbidding in his manners; but he had, as far as I know, no active enemies. I know nothing further of the matter.''

The Coroner: Did your father make any statement to you before he died?

Witness: He mumbled a few words, but I could only catch some allusion to a rat.

The Coroner: What did you understand by that?

Witness: It conveyed no meaning to me. I thought that he was delirious.

The Coroner: What was the point upon which you and your father had this final quarrel?

Witness: I should prefer not to answer.

The Coroner: I am afraid that I must press it.

Witness: It is really impossible for me to tell you. I can assure you that it has nothing to do with the sad tragedy which followed.

The Coroner: That is for the court to decide. I need not point out to you that your refusal to answer will prejudice your case considerably in any future proceedings which may arise.

Witness: I must still refuse.

The Coroner: I understand that the cry of "Cooee" was a common signal between you and your father?

Witness: It was.

The Coroner: How was it, then, that he uttered it before he saw you, and before he even knew that you had returned from Bristol?

Witness (with considerable confusion): I do not know.

A Juryman: Did you see nothing which aroused your suspicions when you returned on hearing the cry and found your father fatally injured?

Witness: Nothing definite.

The Coroner: What do you mean?

Witness: I was so disturbed and excited as I rushed out into the open, that I could think of nothing except of my father. Yet I have a vague impression that as I ran forward something lay upon the ground to the left of me. It seemed to me to be something gray in color, a coat of some sort or a plaid perhaps. When I rose from my father I looked round for it, but it was gone."

"Do you mean that it disappeared before you went for help?"

"Yes, it was gone."

"You cannot say what it was?"

"No, I had a feeling something was there."

"How far from the body?"

"A dozen yards or so."

"And how far from the edge of the wood?"

"About the same."

"Then if it was removed it was while you were within a dozen yards of it?"

"Yes, but with my back towards it."

This concluded the examination of the witness.

"I see," said I as I glanced down the column, "that the coroner in his concluding remarks was rather severe upon young McCarthy. He calls attention, and with reason, to the discrepancy about his father having signaled to him before seeing him, also to his refusal to give details of his conversation with his father, and his singular account of his father's dying words. They are all, as he remarks, very much against the son."

Holmes laughed softly to himself and stretched himself out upon the cushioned seat. "Both you and the coroner have been at some pains," said he, "to single out the very strongest points in the young man's favor. Don't you see that you alternately give him credit for having too much imagination and too little? Too little, if he could not invent a cause of quarrel which would give him the sympathy of the jury; too much, if he evolved from his own inner consciousness anything so *outré* as a dying reference to a rat, and the incident of the vanishing cloth. No, sir, I shall approach this case from the point of view that what this young man says is true, and we shall see whither that hypothesis will lead us. And now here is my pocket Petrarch, and not another word shall I say of this case until we are on the scene of action. We lunch at Swindon, and I see that we shall be there in twenty minutes."

It was nearly four o'clock when we at last, after passing through the beautiful Stroud Valley, and over the broad gleaming Severn, found ourselves at the pretty little country town of Ross. A lean, ferretlike man, furtive and sly-looking, was waiting for us upon the platform. In spite of the light brown dustcoat and leather leggings which he wore in deference to his rustic surroundings, I had no difficulty in recognizing Lestrade, of Scotland Yard. With him we drove to the Hereford Arms where a room had already been engaged for us.

"I have ordered a carriage," said Lestrade as we sat over a cup of tea. "I knew your energetic nature, and that you would not be happy until you had been on the scene of the crime."

"It was very nice and complimentary of you," Holmes answered. "It is entirely a question of barometric pressure."

Lestrade looked startled. "I do not quite follow," he said.

"How is the glass? Twenty-nine, I see. No wind, and not a cloud in the sky. I have a caseful of cigarettes here which need smoking, and the sofa is very much superior to the usual country-hotel abomination. I do not think that it is probable that I shall use the carriage tonight."

Lestrade laughed indulgently. "You have, no doubt, already formed your conclusions from the newspaper," he said. "The case is as plain as a pikestaff, and the more one goes into it the plainer it becomes. Still, of course, one can't refuse a lady, and such a very positive one, too. She had heard of you, and would have your opinion, though I repeatedly told her that there was nothing which you could do which I had not already done. Why, bless my soul! Here is her carriage at the door."

He had hardly spoken before there rushed into the room one of the most lovely young women that I have ever seen in my life. Her violet eyes were shining, her lips parted, a pink flush upon her cheeks, all thought of her natural reserve lost in her overpowering excitement and concern.

"Oh, Mr. Sherlock Holmes!" she cried, glancing from one to the other of us, and finally, with a woman's quick intuition, fastening upon my companion, "I am so glad that you have come. I have driven down to tell you so. I know that James didn't do it. I know it, and I want you to start upon your work knowing it, too. Never let yourself doubt upon that point. We have known each other since we were little children, and I know his faults as no one else does; but he is too tenderhearted to hurt a fly. Such a charge is absurd to anyone who really knows him."

"I hope we may clear him, Miss Turner," said Sherlock Holmes. "You may rely upon my doing all that I can."

"But you have read the evidence. You have formed some conclusion? Do you not see some loophole, some flaw? Do you not yourself think that he is innocent?"

"I think that it is very probable."

"There, now!" she cried, throwing back her head and looking defiantly at Lestrade. "You hear! He gives me hopes."

Lestrade shrugged his shoulders. "I am afraid that my colleague has been a little quick in forming his conclusions," he said.

"But he is right. Oh! I know that he is right. James never did it. And about his quarrel with his father, I am sure that the reason why he would not speak about it to the coroner was because I was concerned in it."

"In what way?" asked Holmes.

"It is no time for me to hide anything. James and his father had many disagreements about me. Mr. McCarthy was very anxious that there should be a marriage between us. James and I have always loved each other as brother and sister; but of course he is young and has seen very little of life yet, and—and—well, he naturally did not wish to do anything like that yet. So there were quarrels, and this, I am sure, was one of them."

"And your father?" asked Holmes. "Was he in favor of such a union?"

"No, he was averse to it also. No one but Mr.

McCarthy was in favor of it.'' A quick blush passed over her fresh young face as Holmes shot one of his keen, questioning glances at her.

"Thank you for this information," said he. "May I see your father if I call tomorrow?"

"I am afraid the doctor won't allow it."

"The doctor?"

"Yes, have you not heard? Poor father has never been strong for years back, but this has broken him down completely. He has taken to his bed, and Dr. Willows says that he is a wreck and that his nervous system is shattered. Mr. McCarthy was the only man alive who had known dad in the old days in Victoria."

"Ha! In Victoria! That is important."

"Yes, at the mines."

"Quite so; at the gold mines, where, as I understand, Mr. Turner made his money."

"Yes, certainly."

"Thank you, Miss Turner. You have been of material assistance to me."

"You will tell me if you have any news tomorrow. No doubt you will go to the prison to see James. Oh, if you do, Mr. Holmes, do tell him that I know him to be innocent."

"I will, Miss Turner."

"I must go home now, for dad is very ill, and he misses me so if I leave him. Goodbye, and God help you in your undertaking." She hurried from the room as impulsively as she had entered, and we heard the wheels of her carriage rattle off down the street.

"I am ashamed of you, Holmes," said Lestrade with dignity after a few minutes' silence.

"Why would you raise up hopes which you are bound to disappoint? I am not over-tender of heart, but I call it cruel."

"I think that I see my way to clearing James McCarthy," said Holmes. "Have you an order to see him in prison?"

"Yes, but only for you and me."

"Then I shall reconsider my resolution about going out. We have still time to take a train to Hereford and see him tonight?"

"Ample."

"Then let us do so. Watson, I fear that you will find it very slow, but I shall only be away a couple of hours."

I walked down to the station with them, and then wandered through the streets of the little town, finally returning to the hotel, where I lay upon the sofa and tried to interest myself in a yellow-backed novel. The puny plot of the story was so thin, however, when compared to the deep mystery through which we were groping, and I found my attention wander so continually from the fiction to the fact, that I at last flung it across the room and gave myself up entirely to a consideration of the events of the day. Supposing that this unhappy young man's story were absolutely true, then what hellish thing, what absolutely unforeseen and extraordinary calamity could have occurred between the time when he parted from his father, and the moment when, drawn back by his screams, he rushed into the glade? It was something terrible and deadly. What could it be? Might not the nature of the injuries reveal something to my medical instincts? I rang the bell and called for the weekly county paper, which contained a verbatim account of the inquest. In the surgeon's deposition it was stated that the posterior third of the left parietal bone and the left half of the occipital bone had been shattered by a heavy blow from a blunt weapon. I marked the spot upon my own head. Clearly such a blow must have been struck from behind. That was to some extent in favor of the accused, as when seen quarreling he was face to face with his father. Still, it did not go for very much, for the older man might have turned his back before the blow fell. Still, it might be worthwhile to call Holmes's attention to it. Then there was the peculiar dying reference to a rat. What could that mean? It could not be delirium. A man dying from a sudden blow does not commonly become delirious. No, it was more likely to be an attempt to explain how he met his fate. But what could it indicate? I cudgeled my brains to find some possible explanation. And then the incident of the gray cloth seen by young McCarthy. If that were true, the murderer must have dropped some part of his dress, presumably his overcoat, in his flight, and must have had the hardihood to return and to carry it away at the instant when the son was kneeling with his back turned not a dozen paces off. What a tissue of mysteries and improbabilities the whole thing was! I did not wonder at Lestrade's opinion, and yet I had so much faith in Sherlock Holmes's insight that I could not lose hope as long as every fresh fact seemed to strengthen his conviction of young McCarthy's innocence.

It was late before Sherlock Holmes returned.

He came back alone, for Lestrade was staying in lodgings in town.

"The glass still keeps very high," he remarked as he sat down. "It is of importance that it should not rain before we are able to go over the ground. On the other hand, a man should be at his very best and keenest for such nice work as that, and I did not wish to do it when fagged by a long journey. I have seen young McCarthy."

"And what did you learn from him?"

"Nothing."

"Could he throw no light?"

"None at all. I was inclined to think at one time that he knew who had done it and was screening him or her, but I am convinced now that he is as puzzled as everyone else. He is not a very quick-witted youth, though comely to look at and, I should think, sound at heart."

"I cannot admire his taste," I remarked, "if it is indeed a fact that he was averse to a marriage with so charming a young lady as this Miss Turner."

"Ah, thereby hangs a rather painful tale. This fellow is madly, insanely, in love with her, but some two years ago, when he was only a lad, and before he really knew her, for she had been away five years at a boarding school, what does the idiot do but get into the clutches of a barmaid in Bristol and marry her at a registry office? No one knows a word of the matter, but you can imagine how maddening it must be to him to be upbraided for not doing what he would give his very eyes to do, but what he knows to be absolutely impossible. It was sheer frenzy of this sort which made him throw his hands up into the air when his father, at their last interview, was goading him on to propose to Miss Turner. On the other hand, he had no means of supporting himself, and his father, who was by all accounts a very hard man, would have thrown him over utterly had he known the truth. It was with his barmaid wife that he had spent the last three days in Bristol, and his father did not know where he was. Mark that point. It is of importance. Good has come out of evil, however, for the barmaid, finding from the papers that he is in serious trouble and likely to be hanged, has thrown him over utterly and has written to him to say that she has a husband already in the Bermuda Dockyard, so that there is really no tie between them. I think that that bit of news has consoled your McCarthy for all that he has suffered.''

"But if he is innocent, who has done it?''

"Ah! Who? I would call your attention very particularly to two points. One is that the murdered man had an appointment with someone at the pool, and that the someone could not have been his son, for his son was away, and he did not know when he would return. The second is that the murdered man was heard to cry 'Cooee!' before he knew that his son had returned. Those are the crucial points upon which the case depends. And now let us talk about George Meredith, if you please, and we shall leave all minor matters until tomorrow.''

There was no rain, as Holmes had foretold, and the morning broke bright and cloudless. At nine o'clock Lestrade called for us with the carriage, and we set off for Hatherley Farm and the Boscombe Pool.

"There is serious news this morning," Lestrade observed. "It is said that Mr. Turner, of the Hall, is so ill that his life is despaired of."

"An elderly man, I presume?" said Holmes.

"About sixty; but his constitution has been shattered by his life abroad, and he has been in failing health for some time. This business has had a very bad effect upon him. He was an old friend of McCarthy's, and, I may add, a great benefactor to him, for I have learned that he gave him Hatherley Farm rent-free."

"Indeed! That is interesting," said Holmes.

"Oh, yes! In a hundred other ways he has helped him. Everybody about here speaks of his kindness to him."

"Really! Does it not strike you as a little singular that this McCarthy, who appears to have had little of his own, and to have been under such obligations to Turner, should still talk of marrying his son to Turner's daughter, who is, presumably, heiress to the estate, and that in such a very cocksure manner, as if it were merely a case of a proposal and all else would follow? It is the more strange, since we know that Turner himself was averse to the idea. The daughter told us as much. Do you not deduce something from that?"

"We have got to the deductions and the inferences," said Lestrade, winking at me. "I find it hard enough to tackle facts, Holmes, without flying away after theories and fancies."

"You are right," said Holmes demurely; "you do find it very hard to tackle the facts."

— "Anyhow, I have grasped one fact which you seem to find it difficult to get hold of," replied Lestrade with some warmth.

"And that is—"

"That McCarthy senior met his death from McCarthy junior and that all theories to the contrary are the merest moonshine."

"Well, moonshine is a brighter thing than fog," said Holmes, laughing. "But I am very much mistaken if this is not Hatherley Farm upon the left."

"Yes, that is it." It was a widespread, comfortable-looking building, two-storied, slate-roofed, with great yellow blotches of lichen upon the gray walls. The drawn blinds and the smokeless chimneys, however, gave it a stricken look, as though the weight of this horror still lay heavy upon it. We called at the door, when the maid, at Holmes's request, showed us the boots which her master wore at the time of his death, and also a pair of the son's, though not the pair which he had then had. Having measured these very carefully from seven or eight different points, Holmes desired to be led to the courtyard, from which we all followed the winding track which led to Boscombe Pool.

Sherlock Holmes was transformed when he was hot upon such a scent as this. Men who had only known the quiet thinker and logician of Baker Street would have failed to recognize him. His face flushed and darkened. His brows were drawn into two hard black lines, while his eyes shone out from beneath them with a steely glitter. His face was bent downward, his shoulders bowed, his lips compressed, and the veins stood out like whipcord in his long, sinewy neck. His nostrils seemed to dilate with a purely animal lust for the chase, and his mind was so absolutely concentrated upon the matter before him that a question or remark fell unheeded upon his ears, or, at the most, only provoked a quick, impatient snarl in reply. Swiftly and silently he made his way along the track which ran through the meadows, and so by way of the woods to the Boscombe Pool. It was damp, marshy ground, as is all that district, and there were marks of many feet, both upon the path and amid the short grass which bounded it on either side. Sometimes Holmes would hurry on, sometimes stop dead, and once he made quite a little detour into the meadow. Lestrade and I walked behind him, the detective indifferent and contemptuous, while I watched my friend with the interest which sprang from the conviction that every one of his actions was directed towards a definite end.

The Boscombe Pool, which is a little reed-girt sheet of water some fifty yards across, is situated at the boundary between the Hatherley Farm and the private park of the wealthy Mr. Turner. Above the woods which lined it upon the farther side we could see the red, jutting pinnacles which marked the site of the rich landowner's dwelling. On the Hatherley side of the pool the woods grew very thick, and there was a narrow belt of sodden grass twenty paces across between the edge of the trees and the reeds which lined the lake. Lestrade showed us the exact spot at which the body had been found, and, indeed, so moist was the ground, that I could plainly see the traces which had been left by the fall of the stricken man. To Holmes, as I could see by his eager face and peering eyes, very many other things were to be read upon the trampled grass. He ran round, like a dog who is picking up a scent, and then turned upon my companion.

"What did you go into the pool for?" he asked.

"I fished about with a rake. I thought there might be some weapon or other trace. But how on earth—"

"Oh, tut, tut! I have no time! That left foot of yours with its inward twist is all over the place. A mole could trace it and there it vanishes among the reeds. Oh, how simple it would all have been had I been here before they came like a herd of buffalo and wallowed all over it. Here is where the party with the lodgekeeper came, and they have covered all tracks for six or eight feet round the body. But here are three separate tracks of the same feet." He drew out a lens and lay down upon his waterproof to have a better view, talking all the time rather to himself than to us. "These are young McCarthy's feet. Twice he was walking, and once he ran swiftly, so that the soles are deeply marked and the heels hardly visible. That bears out his story. He ran when he saw his father on the ground. Then here are the father's feet as he paced up and down. What is this, then? It is the butt-end of the gun as the son stood listening. And this? Ha, ha! What have we here? Tiptoes! Tiptoes! Square, too, quite unusual boots! They come, they go, they come again—of course that was for the cloak. Now where did they come from?'' He ran up and down, sometimes losing, sometimes finding the track until we were well within the edge of the wood and under the shadow of a great beech, the largest tree in the neighborhood. Holmes traced his way to the farther side of this and lay down once more upon his face with a little cry of satisfaction. For a long time he remained there, turning over the leaves and dried sticks, gathering up what seemed to me to be dust into an envelope and examining with his lens not only the ground but even the bark of the tree as far as he could reach. A jagged stone was lying among the moss, and this also he carefully examined and retained. Then he followed a pathway through the wood until he came to the highroad, where all traces were lost.

"It has been a case of considerable interest," he remarked, returning to his natural manner. "I fancy that this gray house on the right must be the lodge. I think that I will go in and have a word with Moran, and perhaps write a little note. Having done that, we may drive back to our luncheon. You may walk to the cab, and I shall be with you presently."

It was about ten minutes before we regained our cab and drove back into Ross, Holmes still carrying with him the stone which he had picked up in the woods.

"This may interest you, Lestrade," he remarked, holding it out. "The murder was done with it."

"I see no marks."

"There are none."

"How do you know, then?"

"The grass was growing under it. It had only lain there a few days. There was no sign of a place whence it had been taken. It corresponds with the injuries. There is no sign of any other weapon."

"And the murderer?"

"Is a tall man, left-handed, limps with the right leg, wears thick-soled shooting boots and a gray cloak, smokes Indian cigars, uses a cigar holder, and carries a blunt penknife in his pocket. There are several other indications, but these may be enough to aid us in our search."

Lestrade laughed. "I am afraid that I am still a skeptic," he said. "Theories are all very well, but we have to deal with a hardheaded British jury."

"*Nous verrons,*" answered Holmes calmly. "You work your own method, and I shall work mine. I shall be busy this afternoon, and shall probably return to London by the evening train."

"And leave your case unfinished?"

"No, finished."

"But the mystery?"

"It is solved."

"Who was the criminal, then?"

"The gentleman I describe."

"But who is he?"

"Surely it would not be difficult to find out. This is not such a populous neighborhood."

Lestrade shrugged his shoulders. "I am a practical man," he said, "and I really cannot undertake to go about the country looking for a left-handed gentleman with a game leg. I should become the laughingstock of Scotland Yard."

"All right," said Holmes quietly. "I have

given you the chance. Here are your lodgings. Goodbye. I shall drop you a line before I leave.''

Having left Lestrade at his rooms, we drove to our hotel, where we found lunch upon the table. Holmes was silent and buried in thought with a pained expression upon his face, as one who finds himself in a perplexing position.

"Look here, Watson," he said when the cloth was cleared; "just sit down in this chair and let me preach to you for a little. I don't know quite what to do, and I should value your advice. Light a cigar and let me expound."

"Pray do so."

"Well, now, in considering this case there are two points about young McCarthy's narrative which struck us both instantly, although they impressed me in his favor and you against him. One was the fact that his father should, according to his account, cry 'Cooee!' before seeing him. The other was his singular dying reference to a rat. He mumbled several words, you understand, but that was all that caught the son's ear. Now from this double point our research must commence, and we will begin it by presuming that what the lad says is absolutely true."

"What of this 'Cooee!' then?"

"Well, obviously it could not have been meant for the son. The son, as far as he knew, was in Bristol. It was mere chance that he was within earshot. The 'Cooee!' was meant to attract the attention of whoever it was that he had the appointment with. But 'Cooee' is a distinctly Australian cry, and one which is used between Australians. There is a strong presumption that the person whom McCarthy expected to meet him at Boscombe Pool was someone who had been in Australia.''

"What of the rat, then?''

Sherlock Holmes took a folded paper from his pocket and flattened it out on the table. "This is a map of the Colony of Victoria,'' he said. "I wired to Bristol for it last night.'' He put his hand over part of the map. "What do you read?''

"ARAT,'' I read.

"And now?'' He raised his hand.

"BALLARAT.''

"Quite so. That was the word the man uttered, and of which his son only caught the last two syllables. He was trying to utter the name of his murderer. So and so, of Ballarat.''

"It is wonderful!'' I exclaimed.

"It is obvious. And now, you see, I had narrowed the field down considerably. The possession of a gray garment was a third point which, granting the son's statement to be correct, was a certainty. We have come now out of mere vagueness to the definite conception of an Australian from Ballarat with a gray cloak.''

"Certainly.''

"And one who was at home in the district, for the pool can only be approached by the farm or by the estate, where strangers could hardly wander.''

"Quite so.''

"Then comes our expedition of today. By an examination of the ground I gained the trifling details which I gave to that imbecile Lestrade, as to the personality of the criminal.''

"But how did you gain them?"

"You know my method. It is founded upon the observation of trifles."

"His height I know that you might roughly judge from the length of his stride. His boots, too, might be told from their traces."

"Yes, they were peculiar boots."

"But his lameness?"

"The impression of his right foot was always less distinct than his left. He put less weight upon it. Why? Because he limped—he was lame."

"But his left-handedness."

"You were yourself struck by the nature of the injury as recorded by the surgeon at the inquest. The blow was struck from immediately behind, and yet was upon the left side. Now, how can that be unless it were by a left-handed man? He had stood behind that tree during the interview between the father and son. He had even smoked there. I found the ash of a cigar, which my special knowledge of tobacco ashes enables me to pronounce as an Indian cigar. I have, as you know, devoted some attention to this, and written a little monograph on the ashes of 140 different varieties of pipe, cigar, and cigarette tobacco. Having found the ash, I then looked round and discovered the stump among the moss where he had tossed it. It was an Indian cigar, of the variety which are rolled in Rotterdam."

"And the cigar holder?"

"I could see that the end had not been in his mouth. Therefore he used a holder. The tip had been cut off, but the cut was not a clean one, so I deduced a blunt penknife."

"Holmes," I said, "you have drawn a net round this man from which he cannot escape, and you have saved an innocent human life as truly as if you had cut the cord which was hanging him. I see the direction in which all this points. The culprit is—"

"Mr. John Turner," cried the hotel waiter, opening the door of our sitting room, and ushering in a visitor.

The man who entered was a strange and impressive figure. His slow, limping step and bowed shoulders gave the appearance of decrepitude, and yet his hard, deep-lined, craggy features, and his enormous limbs showed that he was possessed of unusual strength of body and character. His tangled beard, grizzled hair, and outstanding, drooping eyebrows combined to give an air of dignity and power to his appearance, but his face was of an ashen white, while his lips and the corners of his nostrils were tinged with a shade of blue. It was clear to me at a glance that he was in the grip of some deadly and chronic disease.

"Pray sit down on the sofa," said Holmes gently. "You had my note?"

"Yes, the lodgekeeper brought it up. You said that you wished to see me here to avoid scandal."

"I thought people would talk if I went to the Hall."

"And why did you wish to see me?" He looked across at my companion with despair in his weary eyes, as though his question was already answered.

"Yes," said Holmes, answering the look rather than the words. "It is so. I know all about McCarthy."

The old man sank his face in his hands. "God help me!" he cried. "But I would not have let the young man come to harm. I give you my word that I would have spoken out if it went against him at the Assizes."

"I am glad to hear you say so," said Holmes gravely.

"I would have spoken now had it not been for my dear girl. It would break her heart—it will break her heart when she hears that I am arrested."

"It may not come to that," said Holmes.

"What?"

"I am no official agent. I understand that it was your daughter who required my presence here, and I am acting in her interests. Young McCarthy must be got off, however."

"I am a dying man," said old Turner. "I have had diabetes for years. My doctor says it is a question whether I shall live a month. Yet I would rather die under my own roof than in a jail."

Holmes rose and sat down at the table with his pen in his hand and a bundle of paper before him. "Just tell us the truth," he said. "I shall jot down the facts. You will sign it, and Watson here can witness it. Then I could produce your confession at the last extremity to save young McCarthy. I promise you that I shall not use it unless it is absolutely needed."

"It's as well," said the old man; "it's a question whether I shall live to the Assizes, so it matters little to me, but I should wish to spare Alice the shock. And now I will make the thing clear to you; it has been a long time in the acting, but will not take me long to tell.

"You didn't know this dead man, McCarthy. He was a devil incarnate. I tell you that. God keep you out of the clutches of such a man as he. His grip has been upon me these twenty years. And he has blasted my life. I'll tell you first how I came to be in his power.

"It was in the early '60's at the diggings. I was a young chap then, hot-blooded and reckless, ready to turn my hand at anything; I got among bad companions, took to drink, had no luck with my claim, took to the bush, and in a word became what you would call over here a highway robber. There were six of us, and we had a wild, free life of it, sticking up a station from time to time, or stopping the wagons on the road to the diggings. Black Jack of Ballarat was the name I went under, and our party is still remembered in the colony as the Ballarat Gang.

"One day a gold convoy came down from Ballarat to Melbourne, and we lay in wait for it and attacked it. There were six troopers and six of us, so it was a close thing, but we emptied four of their saddles at the first volley. Three of our boys were killed, however, before we got the swag. I put my pistol to the head of the wagon driver, who was this very man McCarthy. I wish to the Lord that I had shot him then, but I spared him though I saw his wicked little eyes fixed on my face, as though to remember every feature. We got away with the gold, became wealthy men, and made our way over to England without being suspected. There I parted from my old pals and determined to settle down to a quiet and respectable life. I bought this estate, which chanced to be in the market, and I set myself to do a little good with my money, to make up for the way in which I had earned it. I married, too, and though my wife died young she left me my dear little Alice. Even when she was just a baby her wee hand seemed to lead me down the right path as nothing else had ever done. In a word, I turned over a new leaf and did my best to make up for the past. All was going well when McCarthy laid his grip upon me.

"I had gone up to town about an investment, and I met him in Regent Street with hardly a coat to his back or a boot to his foot.

"'Here we are, Jack,' says he, touching me on the arm; 'we'll be as good as a family to you. There's two of us, me and my son, and you can have the keeping of us. If you don't—it's a fine law-abiding country is England, and there's always a policeman within hail.'

"Well, down they came to the west country, there was no shaking them off, and there they have lived rent free on my best land ever since. There was no rest for me, no peace, no forgetfulness; turn where I would, there was his cunning, grinning face at my elbow. It grew worse as Alice grew up, for he soon saw I was more afraid of her knowing my past than of the police. Whatever he wanted he must have, and whatever it was I gave him without question, land, money, houses, until at last he asked a thing which I could not give. He asked for Alice.

"His son, you see, had grown up, and so had my girl, and as I was known to be in weak health, it seemed a fine stroke to him that his lad should step into the whole property. But there I was firm. I would not have his cursed stock mixed with mine; not that I had any dislike to the lad, but his blood was in him, and that was enough. I stood firm. McCarthy threatened. I braved to do his worst. We were to meet at the pool midway between our houses to talk it over.

"When I went down there I found him talking with his son, so I smoked a cigar and waited behind a tree until he should be alone. But as I listened to his talk all that was black and bitter in me seemed to come uppermost. He was urging his son to marry my daughter with as little regard for what she might think as if she were a slut from off the streets. It drove me mad to think that I and all that I held most dear should be in the power of such a man as this. Could I not snap the bond? I was already a dying and desperate man. Though clear of mind and fairly strong of limb, I knew that my own fate was sealed. But my memory and my girl! Both could be saved if I could but silence that foul tongue. I did it, Mr. Holmes. I would do it again. Deeply as I have sinned, I have led a life of martydom to atone for it. But that my girl should be entangled in the same meshes which held me was more than I could suffer. I struck him down with no more compunction than if he had been some foul and venomous beast. His cry brought back his son; but I had gained the cover of the wood, though I was forced to go back to fetch the cloak which I had dropped in my flight. That is the true story, gentlemen, of all that occurred."

"Well, it is not for me to judge you," said Holmes as the old man signed the statement which had been drawn out. "I pray that we may never be exposed to such a temptation."

"I pray not, sir. And what do you intend to do?"

"In view of your health, nothing. You are yourself aware that you will soon have to answer for your deed at a higher court than the Assizes. I will keep your confession, and if McCarthy is condemned I shall be forced to use it. If not, it shall never be seen by mortal eye; and your secret, whether you be alive or dead, shall be safe with us."

"Farewell, then," said the old man solemnly. "Your own deathbeds, when they come, will be the easier for the thought of the peace which you have given to mine." Tottering and shaking in all his giant frame, he stumbled slowly from the room.

"God help us!" said Holmes after a long silence. "Why does fate play such tricks with poor, helpless worms? I never hear of such a case as this that I do not think of Baxter's words, and say, "'There, but for the grace of God, goes Sherlock Holmes.'"

James McCarthy was acquitted at the Assizes on the strength of a number of objections which had been drawn out by Holmes and submitted to the defending counsel. Old Turner lived for seven months after our interview, but he is now dead; and there is every prospect that the son and daughter may come to live happily together in ignorance of the black cloud which rests upon their past.

L.T. Meade and Robert Eustace
Mr. Bovey's Unexpected Will

Amongst all my patients there were none who excited my sense of curiosity like Miss Florence Cusack. I never thought of her without a sense of baffled inquiry taking possession of me, and I never visited her without the hope that someday I should get to the bottom of the mystery which surrounded her.

Miss Cusack was a young and handsome woman. She possessed to all appearance super-abundant health, her energies were extraordinary, and her life completely out of the common. She lived alone in a large house in Kensington Court Gardens, kept a good staff of servants, and went much into society. Her beauty, her sprightliness, her wealth, and, above all, her extraordinary life caused her to be much talked about. As one glanced at this handsome girl with her slender figure, her eyes of the darkest blue, her raven-black hair and clear complexion, it was almost impossible to believe that she was a power in the police courts, and highly respected by every detective in Scotland Yard.

I shall never forget my first visit to Miss Cusack. I had been asked by a brother doctor to see her in his absence. Strong as she was, she was subject to periodical and very acute nervous attacks. When I entered her house she came up to me eagerly.

"Pray do not ask me too many questions or look too curious, Dr. Lonsdale," she said. "I know well that my whole condition is abnormal; but, believe me, I am forced to do what I do."

"What is that?" I inquired.

"You see before you," she continued, with emphasis, "the most acute and, I believe, successful lady detective in the whole of London."

"Why do you lead such an extraordinary life?" I asked.

"To me the life is fraught with the very deepest interest," she answered. "In any case," and now the color faded from her cheeks, and her eyes grew full of emotion, "I have no choice; I am under a promise, which I must fulfill. There are times, however, when I need help—such help as you, for instance, can give me. I have never seen you before, but I like your face. If the time should ever come, will you give me your assistance?"

I asked her a few more questions, and finally agreed to do what she wished.

From that hour Miss Cusack and I became the staunchest friends. She constantly invited me to her house, introduced me to her friends, and gave me her confidence to a marvelous extent.

On my first visit I noticed in her study two enormous brazen bulldogs. They were splendidly cast, and made a striking feature in the arrangements of the room; but I did not pay them any special attention until she happened to mention that there was a story, and a strange one, in connection with them.

"But for these dogs," she said, "and the mystery attached to them, I should not be the woman I am, nor would my life be set apart for the performance of duties at once herculean and ghastly."

When she said these words her face once more turned pale, and her eyes flashed with an ominous fire.

On a certain afternoon in November 1894, I received a telegram from Miss Cusack, asking me to put aside all other work and go to her at once. Handing my patients over to the care of my partner, I started for her house. I found her in her study and alone. She came up to me holding a newspaper in her hand.

"Do you see this?" she asked. As she spoke she pointed to the agony column. The following words met my eyes:

> Send more sand and charcoal dust. Core and mold ready for casting.
> —JOSHUA LINKLATER.

I read these curious words twice, then glanced at the eager face of the young girl.

"I have been waiting for this," she said, in a tone of triumph.

"But what can it mean?" I said. " *'Core and mold ready for casting'*?"

She folded up the paper, and laid it deliberately on the table.

"I thought that Joshua Linklater would say something of the kind," she continued. "I have been watching for a similar advertisement in all the dailies for the last three weeks. This may be of the utmost importance."

"Will you explain?" I said.

"I may never have to explain, or, on the other hand, I may," she answered. "I have not really sent for you to point out this advertisement, but in connection with another matter. Now, pray, come into the next room with me."

She led me into a prettily and luxuriously furnished boudoir on the same floor. Standing by the hearth was a slender fair-haired girl, looking very little more than a child.

"May I introduce you to my cousin, Letitia Ransom?" said Miss Cusack eagerly. "Pray sit down, Letty," she continued, addressing the girl with a certain asperity. "Dr. Lonsdale is the man of all others we want. Now, doctor, will you give me your very best attention, for I have an extraordinary story to relate."

At Miss Cusack's words Miss Ransom immediately seated herself. Miss Cusack favored her with a quick glance, and then once more turned to me.

"You are much interested in queer mental phases, are you not?" she said.

"I certainly am," I replied.

"Well, I should like to ask your opinion with regard to such a will as this."

Once again she unfolded a newspaper, and, pointing to a paragraph, handed it to me. I read as follows:

EXTRAORDINARY TERMS OF A MISER'S WILL

Mr. Henry Bovey, who died last week at a small house at Kew, has left one of the most extraordinary wills on record. During his life his eccentricities and miserly habits were well-known, but this eclipses them all, by the surprising method in which he has disposed of his property.

Mr. Bovey was unmarried, and, as far as can be proved, has no near relations in the world. The small balance at his banker's is to be used for defraying fees, duties, and sundry charges, also any existing debts, but the main bulk of his securities were recently realized, and the money in sovereigns is locked in a safe in his house.

A clause in the will states that there are three claimants to this property, and that the one whose net bodily weight is nearest to the weight of these sovereigns is to become the legatee. The safe containing the property is not to be opened till the three claimants are present; the competition is then to take place, and the winner is at once to remove his fortune.

Considerable excitement has been manifested over the affair, the amount of the fortune being unknown. The date of the competition is also kept a close secret for obvious reasons.

"Well," I said, laying the paper down, "whoever this Mr. Bovey was, there is little doubt that he must have been out of his mind. I never heard of a more crazy idea."

"Nevertheless it is to be carried out," replied Miss Cusack. "Now listen, please, Dr. Lonsdale. This paper is a fortnight old. It is now three weeks since the death of Mr. Bovey, his will has been proved, and the time has come for the carrying out of the competition. I happen to know two of the claimants well, and intend to be present at the ceremony."

I did not make any answer, and after a pause she continued:

"One of the gentlemen who is to be weighed against his own fortune is Edgar Wimburne. He is engaged to my cousin Letitia. If he turns out to be the successful claimant, there is nothing to prevent their marrying at once; if otherwise—" here she turned and looked full at Miss Ransom, who stood up, the color coming and going in her cheeks—"if otherwise, Mr. Campbell Graham has to be dealt with."

"Who is he?" I asked.

"Another claimant, a much older man than Edgar. Nay, I must tell you everything. He is a claimant in a double sense, being also a lover, and a very ardent one, of Letitia's.

"Letty must be saved," she said, looking at me, "and I believe I know how to do it."

"You spoke of three claimants," I interrupted; "who is the third?"

"Oh, he scarcely counts, unless indeed he carries off the prize. He is William Tyndall, Mr. Bovey's servant and retainer."

"And when, may I ask, is this momentous competition to take place?" I continued.

"Tomorrow morning at half past nine, at Mr. Bovey's house. Will you come with us tomorrow, Dr. Lonsdale, and be present at the weighing?"

"I certainly will," I answered; "it will be a novel experience."

"Very well; can you be at this house a little before half past eight, and we will drive straight to Kew?"

I promised to do so, and soon after took my leave. The next day I was at Miss Cusack's house in good time. I found waiting for me Miss Cusack herself, Miss Ransom, and Edgar Wimburne.

A moment or two later we all found ourselves seated in a large landau, and in less than an hour had reached our destination. We drew up at a small dilapidated-looking house, standing in a row of prim suburban villas, and found that Mr. Graham, the lawyer, and the executors had already arrived.

The room into which we had been ushered was fitted up as a sort of study. The furniture was very poor and scanty, the carpet was old, and the only ornaments on the walls were a few tattered prints yellow with age.

As soon as ever we came in, Mr. Southby, the lawyer, came forward and spoke.

"We are met here today," he said, "as you are all of course aware, to carry out the clause of Mr. Bovey's last will and testament. What reasons prompted him to make these extraordinary conditions we do not know; we only know that we are bound to carry them out. In a safe in his bedroom there is, according to his own statement, a large sum of money in gold, which is to be the property of the one of these three gentlemen whose weight shall nearest approach to the weight of the gold. Messrs. Hutchinson and Company have been kind enough to supply one of their latest weighing machines, which has been carefully checked, and now if you three gentlemen will kindly come with me into the next room we will begin the business at once. Perhaps you, Dr. Lonsdale, as a medical man, will be kind enough to accompany us.''

Leaving Miss Cusack and Miss Ransom we then went into the old man's bedroom, where the three claimants undressed and were carefully weighed. I append their respective weights, which I noted down:

Graham	13 stone 9 lbs. 6 oz.
Tyndall	11 stone 6 lbs. 3 oz.
Wimburne	12 stone 11 lbs.

The three candidates having resumed their attire, Miss Cusack and Miss Ransom were summoned, and the lawyer, drawing out a bunch of keys, went across to a large iron safe which had been built into the wall.

We all pressed round him, everyone anxious to get the first glimpse of the old man's hoard. The lawyer turned the key, shot back the lock, and flung open the heavy doors. We found that the safe was literally packed with small canvas bags—indeed, so full was it that as the doors swung open two of the bags fell to the floor with a heavy crunching noise. Mr. Southby lifted them up, and then cutting the strings of one, opened it. It was full of bright sovereigns.

An exclamation burst from us all. If all those bags contained gold there was a fine fortune awaiting the successful candidate! The business was now begun in earnest. The lawyer rapidly extracted bag after bag, untied the string, and shot the contents with a crash into the great copper scale pan, while the attendant kept adding weights to the other side to balance it, calling out the amounts as he did so. No one spoke, but our eyes were fixed as if by some strange fascination on the pile of yellow metal that rose higher and higher each moment.

As the weight reached one hundred and fifty pounds, I heard the old servant behind me utter a smothered oath. I turned and glanced at him; he was staring at the gold with a fierce expression of disappointment and avarice. He at any rate was out of the reckoning, as at eleven stone six, or one hundred and sixty pounds, he could be nowhere near the weight of the sovereigns, there being still eight more bags to untie.

The competition, therefore, now lay between Wimburne and Graham. The latter's face bore strong marks of the agitation which consumed him: the veins stood out like cords on his forehead, and his lips trembled. It would evidently be a near thing, and the suspense was almost intolerable. The lawyer continued to deliberately add to the pile. As the last bag was shot into the scale, the attendant put four ten-pound weights into the other side. It was too much. The gold rose at once. He took one off, and then the two great pans swayed slowly up and down, finally coming to a dead stop.

"Exactly one hundred and eighty pounds, gentlemen," he cried, and a shout went up from us all. Wimburne at twelve stone eleven, or one hundred and seventy-nine pounds, had won.

I turned and shook him by the hand.

"I congratulate you most heartily," I cried. "Now let us calculate the amount of your fortune."

I took a piece of paper from my pocket and made a rough calculation. Taking 56 pounds to the pound avoirdupois, there were at least ten thousand and eighty sovereigns in the scale before us.

"I can hardly believe it," cried Miss Ransom.

I saw her gazing down at the gold; then she looked up into her lover's face.

"Is it true?" she said, panting as she spoke.

"Yes, it is true," he answered. Then he dropped his voice. "It removes all difficulties," I heard him whisper to her.

Her eyes filled with tears, and she turned aside to conceal her emotion.

"There is no doubt whatever as to your ownership of this money, Mr. Wimburne," said the lawyer, "and now the next thing is to ensure its safe transport to the bank."

As soon as the amount of the gold had been made known, Graham, without bidding goodbye to anyone, abruptly left the room, and I assisted the rest of the men in shoveling the sovereigns into a stout canvas bag, which we then lifted and placed in a four-wheeled cab which had arrived for the purpose of conveying the gold to the city.

"Surely someone is going to accompany Mr.

Wimburne?'' said Miss Cusack at this juncture. ''My dear Edgar,'' she continued, ''you are not going to be so mad as to go alone?''

To my surprise, Wimburne colored, and then gave a laugh of annoyance.

''What could possibly happen to me?'' he said. ''Nobody knows that I am carrying practically my own weight in gold into the city.''

''If Mr. Wimburne wishes I will go with him,'' said Tyndall, now coming forward. The old man had to all appearance got over his disappointment, and spoke eagerly.

''The thing is fair and square,'' he added. ''I am sorry I did not win, but I'd rather you had it, sir, than Mr. Graham. Yes, that I would, and I congratulate you, sir.''

''Thank you, Tyndall,'' replied Wimburne, ''and if you like to come with me I shall be very glad of your company.''

The bag of sovereigns being placed in the cab, Wimburne bade us all a hasty goodbye, told Miss Ransom that he would call to see her at Miss Cusack's house that evening, and, accompanied by Tyndall, started off. As we watched the cab turn the corner I heard Miss Ransom utter a sigh.

''I do hope it will be all right,'' she said, looking at me. ''Don't you think it is a risky thing to drive with so much gold through London?''

I laughed in order to reassure her.

''Oh, no, it is perfectly safe,'' I answered, ''safer perhaps than if the gold were conveyed in a more pretentious vehicle. There is nothing to announce the fact that it is bearing ten thousand and eighty sovereigns to the bank.''

A moment or two later I left the two ladies and returned to my interrupted duties. The affair of the weighing, the strange clause in the will, Miss Ransom's eager, pathetic face, Wimburne's manifest anxiety, had all impressed me considerably, and I could scarcely get the affair off my mind. I hoped that the young couple would now be married quickly, and I could not help being heartily glad that Graham had lost, for I had by no means taken to his appearance.

My work occupied me during the greater part of the afternoon, and I did not get back again to my own house until about six o'clock. When I did so I was told to my utter amazement that Miss Cusack had arrived and was waiting to see me with great impatience. I went at once into my consulting room, where I found her pacing restlessly up and down.

"What is the matter?" I asked.

"Matter!" she cried; "have you not heard? Why, it has been cried in the streets already—the money is gone, was stolen on the way to London. There was a regular highway robbery in the Richmond Road, in broad daylight, too. The facts are simply these: Two men in a dogcart met the cab, shot the driver, and after a desperate struggle, in which Edgar Wimburne was badly hurt, seized the gold and drove off. The thing was planned, of course—planned to a moment."

"But what about Tyndall?" I asked.

"He was probably in the plot. All we know is that he has escaped and has not been heard of since."

"But what a daring thing!" I cried. "They will

be caught, of course; they cannot have gone far with the money.''

''You do not understand their tricks, Dr. Lonsdale; but I do,'' was her quick answer, ''and I venture to guarantee that if we do not get that money back before the morning, Edgar Wimburne has seen the last of his fortune. Now, I mean to follow up this business, all night if necessary.''

I did not reply. Her dark, bright eyes were blazing with excitement, and she began to pace up and down.

''You must come with me,'' she continued; ''you promised to help me if the necessity should arise.''

''And I will keep my word,'' I answered.

''That is an immense relief.'' She gave a deep sigh as she spoke.

''What about Miss Ransom?'' I asked.

''Oh, I have left Letty at home. She is too excited to be of the slightest use.''

''One other question,'' I interrupted, ''and then I am completely at your service. You mentioned that Wimburne was hurt.''

''Yes, but I believe not seriously. He has been taken to the hospital. He has already given evidence, but it amounts to very little. The robbery took place in a lonely part of the road, and just for the moment there was no one in sight.''

''Well,'' I said, as she paused, ''you have some scheme in your head, have you not?''

''I have,'' she answered. ''The fact is this: From the very first I feared some such catastrophe

48

as has really taken place. I have known Mr. Graham for a long time, and—distrusted him. He has passed for a man of position and means, but I believe him to be a mere adventurer. There is little doubt that all his future depended on his getting this fortune. I saw his face when the scales declared in Edgar Wimburne's favor—but there! I must ask you to accompany me to Hammersmith immediately. On the way I will tell you more.''

''We will go in my carriage,'' I said. ''It happens to be at the door.''

We started directly. As we had left the more noisy streets Miss Cusack continued:

''You remember the advertisement I showed you yesterday morning?''

I nodded.

''You naturally could make no sense of it, but to me it was fraught with much meaning. This is by no means the first advertisement which has appeared under the name of Joshua Linklater. I have observed similar advertisements, and all, strange to say, in connection with founder's work, appearing at intervals in the big dailies for the last four or five months, but my attention was never specially directed to them until a circumstance occurred of which I am about to tell you.''

''What is that?'' I asked.

''Three weeks ago a certain investigation took me to Hammersmith in order to trace a stolen necklace. It was necessary that I should go to a small pawnbroker's shop—the man's name was Higgins. In my queer work, Dr. Lonsdale, I employ many disguises. That night, dressed quietly as a domestic servant on her evening out, I entered the pawnbroker's. I wore a thick veil and a plainly trimmed hat. I entered one of the little boxes where one stands to pawn goods, and waited for the man to appear.

"For the moment he was engaged, and looking through a small window in the door I saw to my astonishment that the pawnbroker was in earnest conversation with no less a person than Mr. Campbell Graham. This was the last place I should have expected to see Mr. Graham in, and I immediately used both my eyes and ears. I heard the pawnbroker address him as Linklater.

"Immediately the memory of the advertisements under that name flashed through my brain. From the attitude of the two men there was little doubt that they were discussing a matter of the utmost importance, and as Mr. Graham, alias Linklater, was leaving the shop, I distinctly overheard the following words: 'In all probability Bovey will die tonight. I may or may not be successful, but in order to insure against loss we must be prepared. It is not safe for me to come here often—look out for advertisement—it will be in the agony column.'

"I naturally thought such words very strange, and when I heard of Mr. Bovey's death and read an account of the queer will, it seemed to me that I began to see daylight. It was also my business to look out for the advertisement, and when I saw it yesterday morning you may well imagine that my keenest suspicions were aroused. I immediately suspected foul play, but could do nothing except watch and await events. Directly I heard the details of the robbery I wired to the inspector at Hammersmith to have Higgins's house watched. You remember that Mr. Wimburne left Kew in the cab at ten o'clock; the robbery must therefore have taken place some time about ten-twenty. The news reached me shortly after eleven, and my wire was sent off about eleven-fifteen. I mention these hours, as much may turn upon them. Just before I came to you I received a wire from the police station containing startling news. This was sent off about five-thirty. Here, you had better read it.''

As she spoke she took a telegram from her pocket and handed it to me. I glanced over the words it contained.

> Just heard that cart was seen at Higgins's this morning. Man and assistant arrested on suspicion. House searched. No gold there. Please come down at once.

"So they have bolted with it?'' I said.

"That we shall see,'' was her reply.

Shortly afterwards we arrived at the police station. The inspector was waiting for us, and took us at once into a private room.

"I am glad you were able to come, Miss Cusack,'' he said, bowing with great respect to the handsome girl.

"Pray tell me what you have done,'' she answered; "there is not a moment to spare.''

"When I received your wire,'' he said, "I immediately placed a man on duty to watch Higgins's shop, but evidently before I did this the cart must have arrived and gone—the news with regard to the cart being seen outside Higgins's shop did not reach me till four-thirty. On receiving it I immediately arrested both Higgins and his assistant, and we searched the house from attic to cellar, but have found no gold whatever. There is little doubt that the pawnbroker received the gold, and has already removed it to another quarter.''

"Did you find a furnace in the basement?'' suddenly asked Miss Cusack.

"We did,'' he replied, in some astonishment; "but why do you ask?''

To my surprise Miss Cusack took out of her pocket the advertisement which she had shown me that morning and handed it to the inspector. The man read the queer words aloud in a slow and wondering voice:

Send more sand and charcoal dust. Core and mold ready for casting—

JOSHUA LINKLATER.

"I can make nothing of it, miss,'' he said, glancing at Miss Cusack. "These words seem to me to have something to do with founder's work.''

"I believe they have,'' was her eager reply. "It is also highly probable that they have something to do with the furnace in the basement of Higgins's shop.''

"I do not know what you are talking about, miss, but you have something at the back of your head which does not appear.''

"I have," she answered, "and in order to confirm certain suspicions I wish to search the house."

"But the place has just been searched by us," was the man's almost testy answer. "It is impossible that a mass of gold should be there and be overlooked: every square inch of space has been accounted for."

"Who is in the house now?"

"No one; the place is locked up, and one of our men is on duty."

"What size is the furnace?"

"Unusually large," was the inspector's answer.

Miss Cusack gave a smile which almost immediately vanished.

"We are wasting time," she said; "let us go there immediately."

"I must do so, of course, if nothing else will satisfy you, miss; but I assure you—"

"Oh, don't let us waste any more time in arguing," said Miss Cusack, her impatience now getting the better of her. "I have a reason for what I do, and must visit the pawnbroker's immediately."

The man hesitated no longer, but took a bunch of keys down from the wall. A blaze of light from a public house guided us to the pawnbroker's, which bore the well-known sign, the three golden balls. These were just visible through the fog above us. The inspector nodded to the man on duty, and unlocking the door we entered a narrow passage into which the swing doors of several smaller compartments opened. The inspector struck a match, and, lighting the lantern, looked at Miss Cusack, as much as to say, "What do you propose to do now?"

"Take me to the room where the furnace is," said the lady.

"Come this way," he replied.

We turned at once in the direction of the stairs which led to the basement, and entered a room on the right. At the further end was an open range which had evidently been enlarged in order to allow the consumption of a great quantity of fuel, and upon it now stood an iron vessel, shaped as a chemist's crucible. Considerable heat still radiated from it. Miss Cusack peered inside, then she slowly commenced raking out the ashes with an iron rod, examining them closely and turning them over and over. Two or three white fragments she examined with peculiar care.

"One thing at least is abundantly clear," she said at last; "gold has been melted here, and within a very short time; whether it was the sovereigns or not we have yet to discover."

"But surely, Miss Cusack," said the inspector, "no one would be rash enough to destroy sovereigns."

"I am thinking of Joshua Linklater's advertisement," she said. "*'Send more sand and charcoal dust.'* This," she continued, once more examining the white fragments, "is undoubtedly sand."

She said nothing further, but went back to the ground floor and now commenced a systematic search on her own account.

At last we reached the top floor, where the pawnbroker and his assistant had evidently slept. Here Miss Cusack walked at once to the window and flung it open. She gazed out for a minute, and then turned to face us. Her eyes looked brighter than ever, and a certain smile played about her face.

"Well, miss," said the police inspector, "we have now searched the whole house, and I hope you are satisfied."

"I am," she replied.

"The gold is not here, miss."

"We will see," she said. As she spoke she turned once more and bent slightly out, as if to look down through the murky air at the street below.

The inspector gave an impatient exclamation.

"If you have quite finished, miss, we must return to the station," he said. "I am expecting some men from Scotland Yard to go into this affair."

"I do not think they will have much to do," she answered, "except, indeed, to arrest the criminal." As she spoke she leaned a little further out of the window, and then withdrawing her head said quietly, "Yes, we may as well go back now; I have quite finished. Things are exactly as I expected to find them; we can take the gold away with us."

Both the inspector and I stared at her in utter amazement.

"What do you mean, Miss Cusack?" I cried.

"What I say," she answered, and now she gave a light laugh; "the gold is here, close to us; we have only to take it away. Come," she added, "look out, both of you. Why, you are both gazing at it."

I glanced round in utter astonishment. My

expression of face was reproduced in that of the inspector's.

"Look," she said, "what do you call that?" As she spoke she pointed to the sign that hung outside—the sign of the three balls.

"Lean out and feel that lower ball," she said to the inspector.

He stretched out his arm, and as his fingers touched it he started back.

"Why, it is hot," he said; "what in the world does it mean?"

"It means the lost gold," replied Miss Cusack; "it has been cast as that ball. I said that the advertisement would give me the necessary clue, and it has done so. Yes, the lost fortune is hanging outside the house. The gold was melted in the crucible downstairs and cast as this ball between twelve o'clock and four-thirty today. Remember it was after four-thirty that you arrested the pawnbroker and his assistant."

To verify her extraordinary words was the work of a few moments. Owing to its great weight, the inspector and I had some difficulty in detaching the ball from its hook. At the same time we noticed that a very strong stay, in the shape of an iron-wire rope, had been attached to the iron frame from which the three balls hung.

"You will find, I am sure," said Miss Cusack, "that this ball is not of solid gold; if it were, it would not be the size of the other two balls. It has probably been cast round a center of plaster of Paris to give it the same size as the others. This explains the advertisement with regard to the charcoal and sand. A ball of that size in pure gold would weigh nearly three hundred pounds, or twenty stone."

"Well," said the inspector, "of all the curious devices that I have ever seen or heard of, this beats the lot. But what did they do with the real ball? They must have put it somewhere."

"They burned it in the furnace, of course," she answered; "these balls, as you know, are only wood covered with gold paint. Yes, it was a clever idea, worthy of the brain of Mr. Graham; and it might have hung there for weeks and been seen by thousands passing daily, till Mr. Higgins was released from imprisonment, as nothing whatever could be proved against him."

Owing to Miss Cusack's testimony, Graham was arrested that night, and, finding that circumstances were dead against him, he confessed the whole. For long years he was one of a gang of coiners, but managed to pass as a gentleman of position. He knew old Bovey well, and had heard him speak of the curious will he had made. Knowing of this, he determined, at any risk, to secure the fortune, intending, when he had obtained it, to immediately leave the country. He had discovered the exact amount of the money which he would leave behind him, and had gone carefully into the weight which such a number of sovereigns would make. He knew at once that Tyndall would be out of the reckoning, and that the competition would really be between himself and Wimburne. To provide against the contingency of Wimburne's being the lucky man, he had planned the robbery; the gold was to be melted, and made into a real golden ball, which was to hang over the pawnshop until suspicion had died away.

Arnold Bennett

A Bracelet at Bruges

The bracelet had fallen into the canal.

And the fact that the canal was the most picturesque canal in the old Flemish city of Bruges, and that the ripples caused by the splash of the bracelet had disturbed reflections of wondrous belfries, towers, steeples, and other unique examples of Gothic architecture, did nothing whatever to assuage the sudden agony of that disappearance. For the bracelet had been given to Kitty Sartorius by her grateful and lordly manager, Lionel Belmont (U.S.A.), upon the completion of the unexampled run of *The Delminico Doll*, at the Regency Theater, London. And its diamonds were worth five hundred pounds, to say nothing of the gold.

The beautiful Kitty, and her friend Eve Fincastle, the journalist, having exhausted Ostend, had duly arrived at Bruges in the course of their holiday tour. The question of Kitty's jewelry had arisen at the start. Kitty had insisted that she must travel with all her jewels, according to the custom of theatrical stars of great magnitude. Eve had equally insisted that Kitty must travel without jewels, and had exhorted her to remember the days of her simplicity. They compromised. /Kitty was allowed to bring the bracelet, but nothing else save the usual half-dozen rings. The ravishing creature could not have persuaded herself to leave the bracelet behind, because it was so recent a gift and still new and strange and heavenly to her. But, since prudence forbade even Kitty to let the trifle lie about in hotel bedrooms, she was obliged always to wear it. And she had been wearing it this bright afternoon in early October, when the girls, during a stroll, had met one of their new friends, Madame Lawrence, on the world-famous Quai du Rosaire, just at the back of the Hotel de Ville and the Halles.

Madame Lawrence resided permanently in Bruges. She was between twenty-five and forty-five, dark, with the air of continually subduing a natural instinct to dash, and well dressed in black. Equally interested in the peerage and in the poor, she had made the acquaintance of Eve and Kitty at the Hotel de la Grande Place, where she called from time to time to induce English travelers to buy genuine Bruges lace, wrought under her own supervision by her own paupers. She was Belgian by birth, and when complimented on her fluent and correct English, she gave all the praise to her deceased husband, an English barrister. She had settled in Bruges like many people settle there, because Bruges is inexpensive, picturesque, and inordinately respectable. Besides an English church and chaplain, it has two cathedrals and an episcopal palace, with a real bishop in it.

"What an exquisite bracelet! May I look at it?"

It was these simple but ecstatic words, spoken with Madame Lawrence's charming foreign accent, which had begun the tragedy. The three women had stopped to admire the always admirable view from the little quay, and they were leaning over the rails when Kitty unclasped the bracelet for the inspection of the widow. The next instant there was a *plop,* an affrighted exclamation from Madame Lawrence in her native tongue, and the bracelet was engulfed before the very eyes of all three.

The three looked at each other non-plussed. Then they looked around, but not a single person was in sight. Then, for some reason which, doubtless, psychology can explain, they stared hard at the water, though the water there was just as black and foul as it is everywhere else in the canal system of Bruges.

"Surely you've not dropped it!" Eve Fincastle exclaimed in a voice of horror. Yet she knew positively that Madame Lawrence had.

The delinquent took a handkerchief from her muff and sobbed into it. And between her sobs she murmured, "We must inform the police."

"Yes, of course," said Kitty, with the lightness of one to whom a five-hundred-pound bracelet is a bagatelle. "They'll fish it up in no time."

"Well," Eve decided, "you go to the police at

once, Kitty; and Madame Lawrence will go with you, because she speaks French, and I'll stay here to mark the exact spot.''

The other two started, but Madame Lawrence, after a few steps, put her hand to her side. ''I can't'' she sighed, pale. ''I am too upset. I cannot walk. You go with Miss Sartorius,'' she said to Eve, ''and I will stay,'' and she leaned heavily against the railings.

Eve and Kitty ran off, just as if it was an affair of seconds, and the bracelet had to be saved from drowning. But they had scarcely turned the corner, thirty yards away, when they reappeared in company with a high official of police, whom, by the most lucky chance in the world, they had encountered in the covered passage leading to the Place du Borg. This official, instantly enslaved by Kitty's beauty, proved to be the very mirror of politeness and optimism. He took their names and addresses, and a full description of the bracelet, and informed them that at that place the canal was nine feet deep. He said that the bracelet should undoubtedly be recovered on the morrow, but that, as dusk was imminent, it would be futile to commence angling that night. In the meantime the loss should be kept secret; and to make all sure, a succession of gendarmes should guard the spot during the night.

Kitty grew radiant, and rewarded the gallant officer with smiles; Eve was satisfied, and the face of Madame Lawrence wore a less mournful hue.

''And now,'' said Kitty to Madame, when everything had been arranged, and the first of the gendarmes was duly installed at the exact spot against the railings, "you must come and take tea with us in our winter garden; and be gay! Smile: I insist. And I insist that you don't worry."

Madame Lawrence tried feebly to smile.

"You are very good-natured," she stammered.

Which was decidedly true.

II

The winter garden of the Hotel de la Grande Place, referred to in all the hotel's advertisements, was merely the inner court of the hotel, roofed in by glass at the height of the first story. Cane flourished there, in the shape of lounge chairs, but no other plant. One of the lounge chairs was occupied when, just as the carillon in the belfry at the other end of the Place began to play Gounod's "Nazareth," indicating the hour of five o'clock, the three ladies entered the winter garden. Apparently the toilettes of two of them had been adjusted and embellished as for a somewhat ceremonious occasion.

"Lo!" cried Kitty Sartorius, when she perceived the occupant of the chair. "The millionaire! Mr. Thorold, how charming of you to reappear like this! I invite you to tea."

Cecil Thorold rose with appropriate eagerness.

"Delighted!" he said, smiling, and then explained that he had arrived from Ostend about two hours before and had taken rooms in the hotel.

"You knew we were staying here?" Eve asked as he shook hands with her.

"No," he replied; "but I am glad to find you again."

"Are you?" She spoke languidly, but her color heightened and those eyes of hers sparkled.

"Madame Lawrence," Kitty chirruped, "let me present Mr. Cecil Thorold. He is appallingly rich, but we mustn't let that frighten us."

From a mouth less adorable than the mouth of Miss Sartorius such an introduction might have been judged lacking in the elements of good form, but for more than two years now Kitty had known that whatever she did or said was perfectly correct because she did or said it. The new acquaintances laughed amiably and a certain intimacy was at once established.

"Shall I order tea, dear?" Eve suggested.

"No, dear," said Kitty quietly. "We will wait for the Count."

"The Count?" demanded Cecil Thorold.

"The Comte d'Avrec," Kitty explained. "He is staying here."

"A French nobleman, doubtless?"

"Yes," said Kitty; and she added, "you will like him. He is an archaeologist, and a musician—oh, and lots of things!"

"If I am one minute late, I entreat pardon," said a fine tenor voice at the door.

It was the Count. After he had been introduced to Madame Lawrence, and Cecil Thorold had been introduced to him, tea was served.

Now, the Comte d'Avrec was everything that a French count ought to be. As dark as Cecil

Thorold, and even handsomer, he was a little older and a little taller than the millionaire, and a short, pointed, black beard, exquisitely trimmed, gave him an appearance of staid reliability which Cecil lacked. His bow was a vertebrate poem, his smile a consolation for all misfortunes, and he managed his hat, stick, gloves, and cup with the dazzling assurance of a conjurer. To observe him at afternoon tea was to be convinced that he had been specially created to shine gloriously in drawing rooms, winter gardens, and *tables d' hôte*. He was one of those men who always do the right thing at the right moment, who are capable of speaking an indefinite number of languages with absolute purity of accent (he spoke English much better than Madame Lawrence), and who can and do discourse with *verve* and accuracy on all sciences, arts, sports, and religions. In short, he was a phoenix of a count; and this was certainly the opinion of Miss Kitty Sartorius and of Miss Eve Fincastle, both of whom reckoned that what they did not know about men might be ignored. Kitty and the Count, it soon became evident, were mutually attracted; their souls were approaching each other with a velocity which increased inversely as the square of the lessening distance between them. And Eve was watching this approximation with undisguised interest and relish.

Nothing of the least importance occurred, save the Count's marvelous exhibition of how to behave at afternoon tea, until the refection was nearly over; and then, during a brief pause in the talk, Cecil, who was sitting to the left of Madame

Lawrence, looked sharply round at the right shoulder of his tweed coat; he repeated the gesture a second and yet a third time.

"What is the matter with the man?" asked Eve Fincastle. Both she and Kitty were extremely bright, animated, and even excited.

"Nothing. I thought I saw something on my shoulder, that's all," said Cecil. "Ah! It's only a bit of thread." And he picked off the thread with his left hand and held it before Madame Lawrence. "See! It's a piece of thin black silk, knotted. At first I took it for an insect—you know how queer things look out of the corner of your eye. Pardon!" He had dropped the fragment onto Madame Lawrence's black silk dress. "Now it's lost."

"If you will excuse me, kind friends," said Madame Lawrence, "I will go." She spoke hurriedly, and as though in mental distress.

"Poor thing!" Kitty Sartorius exclaimed when the widow had gone. "She's still dreadfully upset"; and Kitty and Eve proceeded jointly to relate the story of the diamond bracelet, upon which hitherto they had kept silence (though with difficulty), out of regard for Madame Lawrence's feelings.

Cecil made almost no comment.

The Count, with the sympathetic excitability of his race, walked up and down the winter garden, asseverating earnestly that such clumsiness amounted to a crime; then he grew calm and confessed that he shared the optimism of the police as to the recovery of the bracelet; lastly he complimented Kitty on her equable demeanor under this affliction.

"Do you know, Count," said Cecil Thorold, later, after they had all four ascended to the drawing room overlooking the Grande Place, "I was quite surprised when I saw at tea that you had to be introduced to Madame Lawrence."

"Why so, my dear Mr. Thorold?" the Count inquired suavely.

"I thought I had seen you together in Ostend a few days ago."

The Count shook his wonderful head.

"Perhaps you have a brother—?" Cecil paused.

"No," said the Count. "But it is a favorite theory of mine that everyone has his double somewhere in the word." Previously the Count had been discussing Planchette—he was a great authority on the supernatural, the sub-conscious, and the subliminal. He now deviated gracefully to the discussion of the theory of doubles.

"I suppose you aren't going out for a walk, dear, before dinner?" said Eve to Kitty.

"No, dear," said Kitty, positively.

"I think I shall," said Eve.

And her glance at Cecil Thorold intimated in the plainest possible manner that she wished not only to have a companion for a stroll, but to leave Kitty and the Count in dual solitude.

"I shouldn't, if I were you, Miss Fincastle," Cecil remarked, with calm and studied blindness. "It's risky here in the evenings—with these canals exhaling miasma and mosquitoes and bracelets and all sorts of things."

"I will take the risk, thank you," said Eve, in an icy tone, and she haughtily departed; she would not cower before Cecil's millions. As for Cecil, he joined in the discussion of the theory of doubles.

III

On the next afternoon but one, policemen were fishing, without success, for the bracelet, and raising from the ancient duct long-buried odors which threatened to destroy the inhabitants of the quay. (When Kitty Sartorius had hinted that perhaps the authorities might see their way to drawing off the water from the canal, the authorities had intimated that the death rate of Bruges was already as high as convenient.) Nevertheless, though nothing had happened, the situation had somehow developed, and in such a manner that the bracelet itself was in danger of being partially forgotten; and of all places in Bruges, the situation had developed on the top of the renowned Belfry which dominates the Grande Place in particular and the city in general.

The summit of the belfry is three hundred and fifty feet high, and it is reached by four hundred and two winding stone steps, each a separate menace to life and limb. Eve Fincastle had climbed those steps alone, perhaps in quest of the view at the top, perhaps in quest of spiritual calm. She had not been leaning over the parapet more than a minute before Cecil Thorold had appeared, his field glasses slung over his shoulder. They had begun to talk a little, but nervously and only in snatches. The wind blew free up there among the forty-eight bells, but the social atmosphere was oppressive.

"The Count is a most charming man," Eve was saying, as if in defense of the Count.

"He is," said Cecil; "I agree with you."

"Oh, no, you don't, Mr. Thorold! Oh, no, you don't."

Then there was a pause, and the twain looked down upon Bruges, with its venerable streets, its grass-grown squares, its waterways, and its innumerable monuments, spread out maplike beneath them in the mellow October sunshine. Citizens passed along the thoroughfare in the semblance of tiny dwarfs.

"If you didn't hate him," said Eve, "you wouldn't behave as you do."

"How do I behave, then?"

Eve schooled her voice to an imitation of jocularity—

"All Tuesday evening, and all day yesterday, you couldn't leave them alone. You know you couldn't."

Five minutes later the conversation had shifted.

"You actually saw the bracelet fall into the canal?" said Cecil.

"I actually saw the bracelet fall into the canal. And no one could have got it out while Kitty and I were away, because we weren't away half a minute."

But they could not dismiss the subject of the Count, and presently he was again the topic.

"Naturally it would be a good match for the

Count—for *any* man," said Eve; "but then it would also be a good match for Kitty. Of course, he is not so rich as some people, but he is rich."

Cecil examined the horizon with his glasses, and then the streets near the Grande Place.

"Rich, is he? I'm glad of it. By the by, he's gone to Ghent for the day, hasn't he?"

"Yes, he went by the 9:27, and returned by the 4:38."

Another pause.

"Well," said Cecil at length, handing the glasses to Eve Fincastle, "kindly glance down there. Follow the line of the Rue St. Nicholas. You see the cream-colored house with the enclosed courtyard? Now, do you see two figures standing together near a door—a man and a woman, the woman on the steps? Who are they?"

"I can't see very well," said Eve.

"Oh, yes, my dear lady, you can," said Cecil. "These glasses are the very best. Try again."

"They look like the Comte d'Avrec and Madame Lawrence," Eve murmured.

"But the Count is on his way from Ghent! I see the steam of the 4:38 over there. The curious thing is that the Count entered the house of Madame Lawrence, to whom he was introduced for the first time the day before yesterday, at ten o'clock this morning. Yes, it would be a very good match for the Count. When one comes to think of it, it usually is that sort of man that contrives to marry a brilliant and successful actress. There! He's just leaving, isn't he? Now let us descend and listen to the recital of his day's doings in Ghent—shall we?"

"You mean to insinuate," Eve burst out in sudden wrath, "that the Count is an—an *adventurer*, and that Madame Lawrence... Oh! Mr. Thorold!" She laughed condescendingly. "This jealousy is too absurd. Do you suppose I haven't noticed how impressed you were with Kitty at the Devonshire Mansion that night, and again at Ostend, and again here? You're simply carried away by jealousy; and you think because you are a millionaire you must have all you want. I haven't the slightest doubt that the Count...."

"Anyhow," said Cecil, "let us go down and hear about Ghent."

His eyes made a number of remarks (indulgent, angry, amused, protective, admiring, perspicacious, puzzled), too subtle for the medium of words.

They groped their way down to earth in silence, and it was in silence that they crossed the Grande Place. The Count was seated on the *terrasse* in front of the hotel, with a liqueur glass before him, and he was making graceful and expressive signs to Kitty Sartorius, who leaned her marvelous beauty out of a first story window. He greeted Cecil Thorold and Eve with an equal grace.

"And how is Ghent?" Cecil inquired.

"Did you go to Ghent, after all, Count?" Eve put in. The Comte d'Avrec looked from one to another, and then, instead of replying, he sipped at his glass. "No," he said, "I didn't go. The rather curious fact is that I happened to meet Madame Lawrence, who offered to show me her collection of lace. I have been an amateur of lace for some years, and really Madame Lawrence's collection is amazing. You have seen it? No? You should do so. I'm afraid I have spent most of the day there."

When the Count had gone to join Kitty in the drawing room, Eve Fincastle looked victoriously at Cecil, as if to demand of him "Will you apologize?"

"My dear journalist," Cecil remarked simply, "you gave the show away."

That evening the continued obstinacy of the bracelet, which still refused to be caught, began at last to disturb the birdlike mind of Kitty Sartorius. Moreover, the secret was out, and the whole town of Bruges was discussing the episode and the chances of success.

"Let us consult Planchette," said the Count. The proposal was received with enthusiasm by Kitty. Eve had disappeared.

Planchette was produced; and when asked if the bracelet would be recovered, it wrote, under the hands of Kitty and the Count, a trembling "Yes." When asked "By whom?" it wrote a word that faintly resembled "Avrec."

The Count stated that he should personally commence dragging operations at sunrise. "You will see," he said, "I shall succeed."

"Let me try this toy, may I?" Cecil asked blandly, and, upon Kitty agreeing, he addressed Planchette in a clear voice, "Now, Planchette, who will restore the bracelet to its owner?"

And Planchette wrote "Thorold," but in characters as firm and regular as those of a copy book.

"Mr. Thorold is laughing at us," observed the Count, imperturbably bland.

"How horrid you are, Mr. Thorold!" Kitty exclaimed.

IV

Of the four persons more or less interested in the affair, three were secretly active that night, in and out of the hotel. Only Kitty Sartorius, chief mourner for the bracelet, slept placidly in her bed. It was towards three o'clock in the morning that a sort of preliminary crisis was reached.

From the multiplicity of doors which ventilate its rooms, one would imagine that the average foreign hotel must have been designed immediately after its architect had been to see a Palais Royal farce, in which every room opens into every other room in every act. The Hotel de la Grande Place was not peculiar in this respect; it abounded in doors. All the chambers on the second story, over the public rooms, fronting the place, communicated one with the next, but naturally most of the communicating doors were locked. Cecil Thorold and the Comte d'Avrec had each a bedroom and a sitting room on that floor. The Count's sitting room adjoined Cecil's; and the door between was locked, and the key in the possession of the landlord.

Nevertheless, at three a.m. this particular door opened noiselessly from Cecil's side, and Cecil entered the domain of the Count. The moon shone, and Cecil could plainly see not only the silhouette of the Belfry across the Place, but also the principal objects within the room. He noticed the table in the middle, the large casy chair turned towards the hearth, the old-fashioned sofa; but not a single article did he perceive which might have been the personal property of the Count. He cautiously passed across the room through the moonlight to the door of the Count's bedroom, which apparently, to his immense surprise, was not only shut, but locked, and the key in the lock on the sitting-room side. Silently unlocking it, he entered the bedroom and disappeared...

In less than five minutes he crept back into the Count's sitting room, closed the door and locked it.

"Odd!" he murmured reflectively; but he seemed quite happy.

There was a sudden movement in the region of the hearth, and a form rose from the armchair. Cecil rushed to the switch and turned on the electric light. Eve Fincastle stood before him. They faced each other.

"What are you doing here at this time, Miss Fincastle?" he asked, sternly. "You can talk freely; the Count will not waken."

"I may ask you the same question," Eve replied, with cold bitterness.

"Excuse me. You may not. You are a woman. This is the Count's room—"

"You are in error," she interrupted him. "It is not the Count's room. It is mine. Last night I told the Count I had some important writing to do, and I asked him as a favor to relinquish this room to me for twenty-four hours. He very kindly consented. He removed his belongings, handed me the key of that door, and the transfer was made in the hotel books. And now," she added, "may I inquire, Mr. Thorold, what you are doing in my room?"

"I—I thought it was the Count's," Cecil faltered, decidedly at a loss for a moment. "In offering my humblest apologies, permit me to say that I admire you, Miss Fincastle."

"I wish I could return the compliment," Eve exclaimed, and she repeated with almost plaintive sincerity: "I do wish I could."

Cecil raised his arms and let them fall to his side.

"You meant to catch me," he said. "You suspected something, then? The 'important writing' was an invention." And he added, with a faint smile: "You really ought not to have fallen asleep. Suppose I had not wakened you?"

"Please don't laugh, Mr. Thorold. Yes, I did suspect. There was something in the demeanor of your servant Lecky that gave me the idea.... I did mean to catch you. Why you, a millionaire, should be a burglar, I cannot understand. I never understood that incident at the Devonshire Mansion; it was beyond me. I am by no means sure that you didn't have a great deal to do with the Rainshore affair at Ostend. But that you should have stooped to slander is the worst. I confess you are a mystery. I confess that I can make no guess at the nature of your present scheme. And what I shall do, now that I have caught you, I don't know. I can't decide; I must think. If, however, anything is missing tomorrow morning, I shall be bound in any case to denounce you. You grasp that?"

"I grasp it perfectly, my dear journalist," Cecil replied. "And something will not improbably be missing. But take the advice of a burglar and a mystery, and go to bed, it is half past three."

And Eve went. And Cecil bowed her out and then retired to his own rooms. And the Count's apartment was left to the moonlight.

V

"Planchette is a very safe prophet," said Cecil to Kitty Sartorius the next morning, "provided it has firm guidance."

They were at breakfast.

"What do you mean?"

"I mean that Planchette prophesied last night that I should restore to you your bracelet. I do."

He took the lovely gewgaw from his pocket and handed it to Kitty.

"Ho-ow did you find it, you dear thing?" Kitty stammered, trembling under the shock of joy.

"I fished it up out—out of the mire by a contrivance of my own."

"But when?"

"Oh! Very early. At three o'clock a.m. You see, I was determined to be first."

"In the dark, then?"

"I had a light. Don't you think I'm rather clever?"

Kitty's scene of ecstatic gratitude does not come into the story. Suffice it to say that not until the moment of its restoration did she realize how precious the bracelet was to her.

It was ten o'clock before Eve descended. She had breakfasted in her room, and Kitty had already exhibited to her the prodigal bracelet.

"I particularly want you to go up the Belfry with me, Miss Fincastle," Cecil greeted her; and his tone was so serious and so urgent that she consented. They left Kitty playing waltzes on the piano in the drawing room.

"And now, O man of mystery?" Eve questioned, when they had toiled to the summit, and saw the city and its dwarfs beneath them.

"We are in no danger of being disturbed here," Cecil began; "but I will make my explanation—the explanation which I certainly owe you—as brief as possible. Your Comte d'Avrec is an adventurer (please don't be angry), and your Madame Lawrence is an adventuress. I knew that I had seen them together. They work in concert, and for the most part make a living on the gaming tables of Europe. Madame Lawrence was expelled from Monte Carlo last year for being too intimate with a croupier. You may be aware that at a roulette table one can do a great deal with the aid of the croupier. Madame Lawrence appropriated the bracelet "on her own," as it were. The Count (he may be a real count, for anything I know) heard first of that enterprise from the lips of Miss Sartorius. He was annoyed, angry—because he was really a little in love with your friend, and he saw golden prospects. It is just this fact—the Count's genuine passion for Miss Sartorius—that renders the case psychologically interesting. To proceed, Madame Lawrence became jealous. The Count spent six hours yesterday in trying to get the bracelet from her, and failed. He tried again last night, and succeeded, but not too easily, for he did not re-enter the hotel till after one o'clock. At first I thought he had succeeded in the daytime, and I had arranged accordingly, for I did not see why he should have the honor and glory of restoring the bracelet to its owner. Lecky and I fixed up a sleeping draft for him. The minor details were simple. When you caught me this morning, the bracelet was in my pocket, and in its stead I had left a brief note for the perusal of the Count, which has had the singular effect of inducing him to decamp; probably he has not gone alone. But isn't it amusing that, since you so elaborately took his sitting room, he will be convinced that you are a party to his undoing— you, his staunchest defender?''

Eve's face gradually broke into an embarrassed smile.

"You haven't explained," she said, "how Madame Lawrence got the bracelet."

"Come over here," Cecil answered. "Take these glasses and look down at the Quai du Rosaire. You see everything plainly?" Eve could, in fact, see on the quay the little mounds of mud which had been extracted from the canal in the quest of the bracelet. Cecil continued: "On my arrival in Bruges on Monday, I had a fancy to climb the Belfry at once. I witnessed the whole scene between you and Miss Sartorius and Madame Lawrence, through my

77

glasses. Immediately your backs were turned, Madame Lawrence, her hands behind her, and her back against the railing, began to make a sort of rapid, drawing up motion with her forearms. Then I saw a momentary glitter....Considerably mystified, I visited the spot after you had left it, chatted with the gendarme on duty and got round him, and then it dawned on me that a robbery had been planned, prepared, and executed with extraordinary originality and ingenuity. A long, thin thread of black silk must have been ready tied to the railing, with perhaps a hook at the other end. As soon as Madame Lawrence held the bracelet, she attached the hook to it and dropped it. The silk, especially as it was the last thing in the world you would look for, would be as good as invisible. When you went for the police, Madame retrieved the bracelet, hid it in her muff, and broke off the silk. Only, in her haste, she left a bit of silk tied to the railing. That fragment I carried to the hotel. All along she must have been a little uneasy about me.... And that's all. Except that I wonder you thought I was jealous of the Count's attentions to your friend.'' He gazed at her admiringly.

"I'm glad you are not a thief, Mr. Thorold," said Eve.

"Well," Cecil smiled, "as for that, I left him a couple of louis for fares, and I shall pay his hotel bill.''

"Why?''

"There were notes for nearly ten thousand francs with the bracelet. Ill-gotten gains, I am sure. A trifle, but the only reward I shall have for my trouble. I shall put them to good use.'' He laughed, serenely gay.

Baroness Orczy

Who Stole the Black Diamonds?

I

"Do you know who that is?" said the man in the corner as he pushed a small packet of photos across the table.

The picture on the top represented an entrancingly beautiful woman, with bare arms and neck, and a profusion of pearl and diamond ornaments about her head and throat.

"Surely this is the Queen of—?"

"Hush!" he broke in abruptly, with mock dismay. "You must mention no names."

"Why not?" I asked, laughing, for he looked so droll in his distress.

"Look closely at the photo," he replied, "and at the necklace and tiara that the lady is wearing."

"Yes," I said. "Well?"

"Do you mean to say you don't recognize them?"

I looked at the picture more closely, and then there suddenly came back to my mind that

79

mysterious story of the Black Diamonds, which had not only bewildered the police of Europe but also some of its diplomats.

"Ah! I see you do recognize the jewels!" said the funny creature after a while. "No wonder! For their design is unique, and photographs of that necklace and tiara were circulated practically throughout all the world.

"Of course I am not going to mention names, for you know very well who the royal heroes of this mysterious adventure were. For the purposes of my narrative, suppose I call them the King and Queen of 'Bohemia.'

"The value of the stones was said to be fabulous, and it was only natural when the King of 'Bohemia' found himself somewhat in want of money—a want which has made itself felt before now with even the most powerful European monarchs—that he should decide to sell the precious trinkets, worth a small kingdom in themselves. In order to be in closer touch with the most likely customers, Their Majesties of 'Bohemia' came over to England during the season of 1902—a season memorable alike for its deep sorrow and its great joy.

"After the sad postponement of the coronation festivities, they rented Eton Chase, a beautiful mansion just outside Chislehurst, for the summer months. There they entertained right royally, for the Queen was very gracious and the King a real sportsman—there also the rumor first got about that His Majesty had decided to sell the world-famous *parure* of Black Diamonds.

"Needless to say, they were not long in the market; quite a host of American millionaires had already coveted them for their wives, and brisk and sensational offers were made to His Majesty's businessman both by letter and telegram.

"At last, however, Mr. Wilson, the multimillionaire, was understood to have made an offer, for the necklace and tiara, of 500,000 pounds, which had been accepted.

"But a very few days later, that is to say, on the Sunday and Monday, 6th and 7th of July, there appeared in the papers the short but deeply sensational announcement that a burglary had occurred at Eton Chase, Chislehurst, the mansion inhabited by Their Majesties the King and Queen of 'Bohemia,' and that among the objects stolen was the famous *parure* of Black Diamonds, for which a bid of half a million sterling had just been made and accepted.

"The burglary had been one of the most daring and most mysterious ones ever brought under the notice of the police authorities. The mansion was full of guests at the time, among whom were many diplomatic notabilities, and also Mr. and Mrs. Wilson, the future owners of the gems; there was also a very large staff of servants. The burglary must have occurred between the hours of 10 and 11:30 P.M., though the precise moment could not be ascertained.

"The house itself stands in the midst of a large garden, and has deep french windows opening out upon the terrace at the back. There are ornamental iron balconies to the windows of the upper floors, and it was to one of these, situated immediately above the dining room, that a rope ladder was found to be attached.

"The burglar must have chosen a moment when the guests were dispersed in the smoking, billiard, and drawing rooms; the servants were having their own meal, and the dining room was deserted. He must have slung his rope ladder, and entered Her Majesty's own bedroom by the window which—as the night was very warm—had been left open. The jewels were locked up in a small iron box which stood upon the dressing table, and the burglar took the box bodily away with him, and then, no doubt, returned the way he came.

"The wonderful point in this daring attempt was the fact that most of the windows on the ground floor were slightly open that night, that the rooms themselves were filled with guests, and that the dining room was not empty for more than a few minutes at a time as the servants were still busy clearing away after dinner.

"At nine o'clock some of the younger guests had strolled out onto the terrace, and the last of these returned to the drawing room at ten o'clock; at half past eleven one of the servants caught sight of the rope ladder in front of one of the dining room windows, and the alarm was given.

"All traces of the burglar, however, and of his princely booty had completely disappeared."

II

"Not only did this daring burglary cause a great deal of excitement," continued the man in the corner, "but it also roused a good deal of sympathy in the public mind for the King and Queen of 'Bohemia,' who thus found their hope of raising half a million sterling suddenly dashed to the ground. The loss to them would, of course, be irreparable.

"Matters were, however, practically at a stand-still, all inquiries from enterprising journalists only eliciting the vague information that the police 'held a clue.' We all know what that means. Then all at once a wonderful rumor got about.

"Goodness only knows how these rumors originate—sometimes solely in the imagination of the man in the street. In this instance, certainly, that worthy gentleman had a very sensational theory. It was, namely, rumored all over London that the clue which the police held pointed to no less a person than Mr. Wilson himself.

"What had happened was this: Minute inquiries on the part of the most able detectives of Scotland Yard had brought to light the fact that the burglary at Eton Chase must have occurred precisely between ten minutes and a quarter past eleven; at every other moment of the entire evening somebody or other had observed either the terrace or the dining-room windows.

"I told you that until ten o'clock some of Their Majesties' guests were walking up and down the terrace; between ten and half past, servants were clearing away in the dining room, and here it was positively ascertained beyond any doubt that no burglar could have slung a rope ladder and climbed up it immediately outside those windows, for one or other of the six servants engaged in clearing away the dinner must of necessity have caught sight of him.

"At half past ten John Lucas, the head gardener, was walking through the gardens with a dog at his heels, and did not get back to the lodge until just upon eleven. He certainly did not go as far as the terrace, and as that side of the house was in shadow he could not say positively whether the ladder was there or not, but he certainly did assert most emphatically that there was no burglar about the *grounds* then, for the dog was a good watchdog and would have barked if any stranger was about. Lucas took the dog in with him and gave him a bit of supper, and only fastened him to his kennel outside at a quarter past eleven.

"Surmising, therefore, that at half past ten, when John Lucas started on his round, the deed was not yet done, that quarter of an hour would give the burglar the only possible opportunity of entering the premises *from the outside*, without being barked at by the dog. Now, during most of that same quarter of an hour, His Majesty the King of 'Bohemia' himself had retired into a small library with his private secretary, in order to glance through certain dispatches which had arrived earlier in the evening.

"The window of this library was immediately next to the one outside which the ladder was found, and both the secretary and His Majesty himself think that they would have seen something or heard a noise if the rope ladder had been swung while they were in the room. They both, however, returned to the drawing room at ten minutes past eleven.

"And here," continued the man in the corner, rubbing his long, bony fingers together, "arose the neatest little complication I have ever come across in a case of this kind. His Majesty had, it appears, privately made up his mind to accept Mr. Wilson's bid, but the transaction had not yet been completed. Mr. Wilson and his wife came down to stay at Eton Chase on 29th June, and directly they arrived many of those present noticed that Mr. Wilson was obviously repenting of his bargain. This impression had deepened day by day, Mrs. Wilson herself often throwing out covert hints about 'fictitious value' and 'fancy prices for merely notorious trinkets.' In fact it became very obvious that the Wilsons were really seeking a loophole for evading the conclusion of the bargain.

"On the memorable evening of 5th July, Mrs. Wilson had been forced to retire to her room early in the evening owing, she said, to a bad headache; her room was in the west wing of the Chase, and opened out on the same corridor as the apartments of Her Majesty the Queen. At half past eleven Mrs. Wilson rang for her maid, Mary Pritchard, who, on entering her mistress's room, met Mr. Wilson just coming out of it, and the girl heard him say: 'Oh, don't worry! I'll have the whole reset when we get back.'

"The detectives, on the other hand, had obtained information that two or three days previously Mr. Wilson had sustained a very severe loss on the 'Change, and that he had subsequently remarked to two or three business friends that the Black Diamonds had become a luxury which he had no right to afford.

"Be that as it may, certain it is that within a week of the notorious burglary the rumor was current in every club in London that James S. Wilson, the reputed American millionaire, having found himself unable to complete the purchase of the Black Diamonds, had found this other very much less legitimate means of gaining possession of the gems.

"You must admit that the case looked black

enough against him—all circumstantial, of course, for there was absolutely nothing to prove that he had the jewels in his possession; in fact no trace of them whatever had been found, but the public argued that Mr. Wilson would lie low with them for a while, and then have them reset when he returned to America.

"Of course ugly rumors of that description don't become general about a man without his getting some inkling of them. Mr. Wilson very soon found his position in London absolutely intolerable. His friends ignored him at the club, ladies ceased to call upon his wife, and one fine day he was openly cut by Lord Barnsdale, M.F.H., in the hunting field.

"Then Mr. Wilson thought it high time to take action. He placed the whole matter in the hands of an able, if not very scrupulous, solicitor, who promised within a given time to find him a defendant with plenty of means, against whom he could bring a sensational libel suit with thundering damages.

"The solicitor was as good as his word. He bribed some of the waiters at the Carlton, and so laid his snares that, within six months, Lord and Lady Barnsdale had been overheard to say in public what everybody now thought in private, namely that Mr. James S. Wilson, finding himself unable to purchase the celebrated Black Diamonds, had thought it more profitable to steal them.

"Two days later Mr. James S. Wilson entered an action in the High Court for slander against Lord and Lady Barnsdale, claiming damages to the tune of 50,000 pounds."

"Still the mystery of the lost jewels was no nearer to its solution. Their Majesties the King and Queen of 'Bohemia' had left England soon after the disastrous event which deprived them of what amounted to a small fortune.

"It was expected that the sensational slander case would come on in the autumn, or rather more than sixteen months after the mysterious disappearance of the Black Diamonds.

"This last season was not a very brilliant one, if you remember; the wet weather, I believe, had quite a good deal to do with the fact. Nevertheless London, that great world center, was as usual full of distinguished visitors, among whom Mrs. Vanderdellen, who arrived the second week in July, was perhaps the most interesting.

"Her enormous wealth spread a positive halo round her, it being generally asserted that she was the richest woman in the world. Add to this that she was young, strikingly handsome, and a widow, and you will easily understand what a furor her appearance during this London season caused in all high social circles.

"Though she was still in slight mourning for her husband, she was asked everywhere, went everywhere, and was courted and admired by everybody, including some of the highest in the land; her dresses and jewelry were the talk of the ladies' papers, her style and charm the gossip of all the clubs. And no doubt that, although the July evening court promised to be very brilliant, everyone thought that it would be doubly so, since Mrs.

Vanderdellen had been honored with an invitation and would presumably be present.

"I like to picture to myself that scene at Buckingham Palace," continued the man in the corner as his fingers toyed lovingly with a beautiful and brand-new bit of string. "Of course I was not present actually, but I can see it all before me: the lights, the crowds, the pretty women, the glistening diamonds; then, in the midst of the chatter, a sudden silence fell as Mrs. Vanderdellen was announced.

"All women turned to look at the beautiful American as she entered, because her dress—on this her first appearance at the English Court—was sure to be a vision of style and beauty. But for once nobody noticed the dress from Felix, nobody even gave a glance at the exquisitely lovely face of the wearer. Everyone's eyes had fastened on one thing only, and everyone's lips framed but one exclamation, and that an 'Oh!' half of amazement and half of awe.

"For round her neck and upon her head Mrs. Vanderdellen was wearing a gorgeously magnificent *parure* composed of black diamonds."

IV

"I don't know how the case of Wilson *v.* Barnsdale was settled, for it never came into court. There were many people in London who owed the Wilsons an apology, and it is to be hoped that these were tendered in full.

"As for Mrs. Vanderdellen, she seemed quite unaware why her appearance at Their Majesties' Court had caused so much sensation. No one, of course, broached the subject of the diamonds to her, and she no doubt attributed those significant 'Oh's' to her own dazzling beauty.

"The next day, however, Detective Marsh of Scotland Yard had a very difficult task before him. He had to go and ask a beautiful, rich, and refined woman how she happened to be in possession of stolen jewelry.

"Luckily for Marsh, however, he had to deal with a woman who was also charming, and who met his polite inquiry with an equally pleasant reply:

"'My husband gave me the Black Diamonds,' she said, 'a year ago, on his return from Europe. I had them set in Vienna last spring, and wore them for the first time last night. Will you please tell me the reason for this strange inquiry?'

"'Your husband?' echoed Marsh, ignoring her question, 'Mr. Vanderdellen?'

"'Oh yes,' she replied sweetly. 'I dare say you have never heard of him. His name is very well-known in America, where they call him the "Petrol King." One of his hobbies was the collection of gems, which he was very fond of seeing me wear, and he gave me some magnificent jewels. The Black Diamonds certainly are very handsome. May I now request you to tell me,' she repeated, with a certain assumption of hauteur, 'the reason for all these inquiries?'

"'The reason is simple enough, madam,' replied the detective abruptly. 'Those diamonds were the property of Her Majesty the Queen of "Bohemia," and were stolen from Their Majesties' residence, Eton Chase, Chislehurst, on the 5th of July last year.'

"'Stolen!' she repeated, aghast and obviously incredulous.

"'Yes, stolen,' said old Marsh. 'I don't wish to distress you unnecessarily, madam, but you will see how imperative it is that you should place me in immediate communication with Mr. Vanderdellen, as an explanation from him has become necessary.'

"'Unfortunately that is impossible,' said Mrs. Vanderdellen, who seemed under the spell of a strong emotion.

"'Impossible?'

"'Mr. Vanderdellen has been dead just over a year. He died three days after his return to New York, and the Black Diamonds were the last present he ever made me.'

"There was a pause after that. Marsh—experienced detective though he was—was literally at his wits' end what to do. He said afterwards that Mrs. Vanderdellen, though very young and frivolous outwardly, seemed at the same time an exceedingly shrewd, far-seeing businesswoman. To begin with, she absolutely refused to have the matter hushed up, and to return the jewels until their rightful ownership had been properly proved.

"'It would be tantamount,' she said, 'to admitting that my husband had come by them unlawfully.'

"At the same time she offered the princely reward of 10,000 pounds to anyone who found the true solution of the mystery; for, mind you, the late Mr. Vanderdellen sailed from Le Havre for New York on 8th July, 1902, that is to say, three clear days after the theft of the diamonds from Eton

Chase, and he presented his wife with the loose gems immediately on his arrival in New York. Three days after that he died.

"It was difficult to suppose that Mr. Vanderdellen purchased those diamonds not knowing that they must have been stolen, since directly after the burglary the English police telegraphed to all their continental colleagues, and within four-and-twenty hours a description of the stolen jewels was circulated throughout Europe.

"It was, to say the least of it, very strange that an experienced businessman and shrewd collector like Mr. Vanderdellen should have purchased such priceless gems without making some inquiries as to their history, more especially as they must have been offered to him in a more or less 'hole-in-the-corner' way.

"Still, Mrs. Vanderdellen stuck to her guns, and refused to give up the jewels pending certain inquiries she wished to make. She declared that she wished to be sued for the diamonds in open court, charged with willfully detaining stolen goods if necessary, for the more publicity was given to the whole affair the better she would like it, so firmly did she believe in her husband's innocence.

"The matter was indeed brought to the High Court, and the sensational action brought against Mrs. Vanderdellen by the representative of His Majesty the King of 'Bohemia' for the recovery of the Black Diamonds is, no doubt, still fresh in your memory.

"No one was allowed to know what witnesses Mrs. Vanderdellen would bring forward in her defense. She had engaged the services of Sir Arthur

Inglewood and of some of the most eminent counsel at the Bar. The court was packed with the most fashionable crowd ever seen inside the Law Courts; and both days that the action lasted Mrs. Vanderdellen appeared in exquisite gowns and ideal hats.

"The evidence for the royal plaintiff was simple enough. It all went to prove that the very day after the burglary not a jeweler, pawnbroker, or diamond merchant throughout the whole of Europe could have failed to know that a unique *parure* of black diamonds had been stolen and would probably be offered for sale. The Black Diamonds in themselves, and out of their setting, were absolutely unique, and if the late Mr. Vanderdellen purchased them in Paris from some private individual he must at least have very strongly suspected that they were stolen.

"Throughout the whole of that first day Mrs. Vanderdellen sat in court, absolutely calm and placid. She listened to the evidence, made little notes and chatted with two or three American friends—elderly men—who were with her.

"Then came the turn of the defense.

"Everybody had expected something sensational, and listened more eagerly than ever as the name of Mr. Albert V.B. Sedley was called. He was a tall, elderly man, the regular type of American with his nasal twang and reposeful manner.

"His story was brief and simple. He was a great friend of the late Mr. Vanderdellen, and had gone on a European tour with him in the early spring of 1902. They were together in Vienna in the month of March, staying at the Hotel Imperial, when one day Venderdellen came to his room with a remarkable story.

"'He told me,' continued Mr. Albert V.B. Sedley, 'that he had just purchased some very beautiful diamonds, which he meant to present to his wife on his return to New York. He would not tell me where he bought them, nor would he show them to me, but he spoke about the beauty and rarity of the stones, which were that rarest of all things, beautiful black diamonds.

"'As the whole story sounded to me a little bit queer and mysterious I gave him a word of caution, but he was quite confident as to the integrity of the vendor of the jewels, since the latter had made a somewhat curious bargain. Vanderdellen was to have the diamonds in his keeping for three months without paying any money, merely giving a formal receipt for them; then, if after three months he was quite satisfied with his bargain, and there had been no suspicion or rumor of any kind that the diamonds were stolen, then only was the money, 500,000 pounds, to be paid.

"'Vanderdellen thought this very fair and aboveboard, and so it sounded to me. The only thing I didn't like about it all was that the vendor had given what I thought was a false name and no address. The money was to be paid over to him in French notes when the three months had expired, at a hotel in Paris where Vanderdellen would be staying at the time, and where he would call for it.

"'I heard nothing more about the mysterious diamonds and their still more mysterious vendor,' continued Mr. Sedley, amidst intense excitement, 'for Vanderdellen and I soon parted company after that, he going one way and I another. But at the beginning of July I met him in Paris, and on the 4th dined with him at the Elysée Palace Hotel, where he was staying.

"'Mr. Cornelius R. Shee was there too, and Vanderdellen related to him during dinner the history of his mysterious purchase of the Black Diamonds, adding that the vendor had called upon him that very day as arranged, and that he (Vanderdellen) had had no hesitation in handing him over the agreed price of 500,000 pounds, which he thought a very low one. Both Mr. Shee and I agreed that the whole thing must have been clear and aboveboard, for jewels of such fabulous value could not have been stolen since last spring without the hue and cry being in every paper in Europe.

"'It is my opinion, therefore,' said Mr. Albert V.B. Sedley, at the conclusion of this remarkable evidence, 'that Mr. Vanderdellen bought those diamonds in perfect good faith. He would never have wittingly subjected his wife to the indignity of being seen in public with stolen jewels round her neck. If after 5th July he did happen to hear that a *parure* of black diamonds had been stolen in England at that date, he could not possibly think that there could be the slightest connection between these and those he had purchased more than three months ago.'

"And, amidst indescribable excitement, Mr. Albert V.B. Sedley stepped back into his place.

"That he had spoken the truth from beginning to end no one could doubt for a single moment. His own social position, wealth, and important commercial reputation placed him above any suspicion of committing perjury, even for the sake of a dead friend. Moreover, the story told by Vanderdellen at the dinner in Paris was corroborated by Mr. Cornelius R. Shee in every point.

"But there! A dead man's words are *not* evidence in a court of law. Unfortunately, Mr. Vanderdellen had not shown the diamonds to his friends at the time. He had certainly drawn enormous sums of money from his bank about the end of June and beginning of July, amounting in all to just over a million sterling; and there was nothing to prove which special day he had paid away a sum of 500,000 pounds, whether *before* or *after* the burglary at Eton Chase.

"He had made extensive purchases in Paris of pictures, furniture, and other works of art, all of priceless value, for the decoration of his new palace on Fifth Avenue, and no diary of private expenditure was produced in court. Mrs. Vanderdellen herself had said that after her husband's death, as all his affairs were in perfect order, she had destroyed his personal and private diaries.

"Thus the counsel for the plaintiff was able to demolish the whole edifice of the defense bit by bit, for it rested on but very ephemeral foundations: a story related by a dead man.

"Judgment was entered for the plaintiff, although everyone's sympathy, including that of judge and jury, was entirely for the defendant, who had so nobly determined to vindicate her husband's reputation.

"But Mrs. Vanderdellen proved to the last that she was no ordinary, everyday woman. She had kept one final sensation up her sleeve. Two days after she had legally been made to give up the Black Diamonds, she offered to purchase them back for

500,000 pounds. Her bid was accepted and, during last autumn, on the occasion of the last royal visit to London and the consequent grand society functions, no one was more admired, more feted and envied, than beautiful Mrs. Vanderdellen as she entered a drawing room exquisitely gowned, and adorned with the *parure* of which an empress might have been proud.''

The man in the corner had paused, and was idly tapping his fingers on the marble-topped table of the A.B.C. shop.

"It was a curious story, wasn't it?" said the funny creature after a while. "More like a romance than a reality.''

"It is absolutely bewildering," I said.

"What is your theory?" he asked.

"What about?" I retorted.

"Well, there are so many points, aren't there, of which only one is quite clear; namely, that the *parure* of Black Diamonds disappeared from Eton Chase, Chislehurst, on 5th July, 1902, and that the next time they were seen they were on the neck and head of Mrs. Vanderdellen, the widow of one of the richest men of modern times, whilst the story of how her husband came by them was, to all intents and purposes, *legally* disbelieved.''

"Then," I argued, "the only logical conclusion to arrive at in all this is that the Black Diamonds, owned by His Majesty the King of 'Bohemia,' were not unique, and that Mr. Vanderdellen bought some duplicate ones.''

"If you knew anything about diamonds," he said irritably, "you would also know that your statement is an absurdity. There are no such things as 'duplicate' diamonds.''

"Then what *is* the only logical conclusion to arrive at?'' I retorted, for he had given up playing with the photos and was twisting and twining that bit of string as if his brain was contained inside it and he feared it might escape.

"Well, to me," he said, "the only logical conclusion of the affair is that the Black Diamonds which Mrs. Vanderdellen wore were the only and original ones belonging to the Crown of 'Bohemia.'

"Then you think that a man in Mr. Vanderdellen's position would have been fool enough to buy gems worth 500,000 pounds at the very moment when there was a hue and cry for them all over Europe?''

"No, I don't," he replied quietly.

"But then—" I began.

"No," he repeated once again as his long fingers completed knot number one in that eternal piece of string. "The Black Diamonds which Mrs. Vanderdellen wore were bought by her husband in all good faith from the mysterious vendor in Vienna in March 1902.''

"Impossible!" I retorted. "Her Majesty the Queen of 'Bohemia' wore them regularly during the months of May and June, and they were stolen from Eton Chase on 5th July.''

"Her Majesty the Queen of 'Bohemia' wore a *parure* of Black Diamonds during those months, and those certainly were stolen on 5th July," he said excitedly; "but what was there to prove that *those* were the genuine stones?''

"Why—!" I ejaculated.

"Point No. 2," he said, jumping about like a monkey on a stick; "although Mr. Wilson was acknowledged to be innocent of the theft of the diamonds, isn't it strange that no one has ever been proved guilty of it?"

"But I don't understand—"

"Yes it is simple as daylight. I maintain that His Majesty the King of 'Bohemia,' being short, very short, of money, decided to sell the celebrated Black Diamonds. To avoid all risks, the stones are taken out of their settings, and a trusted and secret emissary is then deputed to find a possible purchaser; his choice falls on the multimillionaire Vanderdellen, who is traveling in Europe, is a noted collector of rare jewelry and has a beautiful young wife—three attributes, you see, which make him a very likely purchaser.

"The emissary then seeks him out and offers him the diamonds for sale. Mr. Vanderdellen at first hesitates, wondering how such valuable gems had come into the vendor's possession, but the bargain suggested by the latter—the three months during which the gems are to be held on trust by the purchaser—seems so fair and aboveboard that Mr. Vanderdellen's objections fall to the ground; he accepts the bargain, and three months later completes the purchase."

"But I don't understand," I repeated again, more bewildered than before. "You say the King of 'Bohemia' sold the loose gems originally to Mr. Vanderdellen; then what about the *parure* worn by the Queen and offered for sale to Mr. and Mrs. Wilson? What about the theft at Eton Chase?"

"Point No. 3," he shrieked excitedly as another

series of complicated knots went to join its fellows. "I told you that the King of 'Bohemia' was *very* short of money—everyone knows *that*. He sells the Black Diamonds to Mr. Vanderdellen, but, before he does it, he causes duplicates of them to be made, but this time in exquisite, beautiful, perfect Parisian imitation, and has these mounted into the original settings by some trusted man who, you may be sure, was well paid to hold his tongue. Then it is given out that the *parure* is for sale; a purchaser is found, and a few days later the false diamonds are stolen."

"By whom?"

"By the King of 'Bohemia's' valued and trusted friend, who has helped in the little piece of villainy throughout; it is he who drops a rope ladder through Her Majesty's bedroom window onto the terrace below, and then hands the imitation *parure* to his royal master, who sees to its complete destruction and disappearance. Then there is a hue and cry for the *real* stones, and after a year or so they are found on the person of a lady who is legally forced to give them up. And thus His Majesty the King of "Bohemia" got one solid million for the Black Diamonds, instead of half that sum, for, if Mrs. Vanderdellen had not purchased the jewels, someone else would have done so."

And he was gone, leaving me to gaze at the pictures of three lovely women, and wondering if indeed it was the royal lady herself who could best solve the mystery of who stole the Black Diamonds.

R. Austin Freeman

The Blue Sequin

Thorndyke stood looking up and down the platform with anxiety that increased as the time drew near for the departure of the train.

"This is very unfortunate," he said, reluctantly stepping into an empty smoking compartment as the guard executed a flourish with his green flag. "I am afraid we have missed our friend." He closed the door and, as the train began to move, thrust his head out of the window.

"Now I wonder if that will be he," he continued. "If so he has caught the train by the skin of his teeth, and is now in one of the rear compartments."

The subject of Thorndyke's speculations was Mr. Edward Stopford, of the firm of Stopford & Myers, of Portugal Street, solicitors, and his connection with us at present arose out of a telegram that had reached our chambers on the preceding evening. It was reply paid, and ran thus:

Can you come here tomorrow to direct defense? Important case. All costs undertaken by us.—STOPFORD & MYERS.

Thorndyke's reply had been in the affirmative, and early on this present morning a further telegram—evidently posted overnight—had been delivered:

Shall leave for Woldhurst by 8:25 from Charing Cross. Will call for you if possible.
                                —EDWARD STOPFORD.

He had not called, however, and, since he was unknown personally to us both, we could not judge whether or not he had been among the passengers on the platform.

"It is most unfortunate," Thorndyke repeated, "for it deprives us of that preliminary consideration of the case which is so invaluable." He filled his pipe thoughtfully and, having made a fruitless inspection of the platform at London Bridge, took up the paper that he had bought at the bookstall, and began to turn over the leaves, running his eye quickly down the columns, unmindful of the journalistic baits in paragraph or article.

"It is a great disadvantage," he observed, while still glancing through the paper, "to come plump into an inquiry without preparation—to be confronted with the details before one has a chance of considering the case in general terms. For instance...."

He paused, leaving the sentence unfinished,

and as I looked up inquiringly I saw that he had turned over another page, and was now reading attentively.

"This looks like our case, Jervis," he said presently, handing me the paper and indicating a paragraph at the top of the page. It was quite brief, and was headed "Terrible Murder in Kent," the account being as follows:

A shocking crime was discovered yesterday morning at the little town of Woldhurst, which lies on the branch line from Halbury Junction. The discovery was made by a porter who was inspecting the carriages of the train which had just come in. On opening the door of a first-class compartment, he was horrified to find the body of a fashionably dressed woman stretched upon the floor. Medical aid was immediately summoned, and on the arrival of the divisional surgeon, Dr. Morton, it was ascertained that the woman had not been dead more than a few minutes.

The state of the corpse leaves no doubt that a murder of a most brutal kind had been perpetrated, the cause of death being a penetrating wound of the head, inflicted with some pointed implement which must have been used with terrible violence since it had perforated the skull and entered the brain. That robbery was not the motive of the crime is made clear by the fact that an expensively fitted dressing bag was found on the rack, and that the dead woman's jewelry, including several valuable diamond rings, was untouched. It is rumored that an arrest has been made by the local police.

"A gruesome affair," I remarked as I handed back the paper, "but the report does not give us much information."

"It does not," Thorndyke agreed, "and yet it gives us something to consider. Here is a perforating wound of the skull, inflicted with some pointed implement—that is, assuming that it is not a bullet wound. Now, what kind of implement would be capable of inflicting such an injury? How would such an implement be used in the confined space of a railway carriage, and what sort of person would be in possession of such an implement? These are preliminary questions that are worth considering, and I commend them to you, together with the further problems of the possible motive—excluding robbery—and any circumstances other than murder which might account for the injury."

"The choice of suitable implements is not very great," I observed.

"It is very limited, and most of them, such as a plasterer's pick or a geological hammer, are associated with certain definite occupations. You have a notebook?"

I had, and, accepting the hint, I produced it and pursued my further reflections in silence, while my companion, with his notebook also on his knee, gazed steadily out of the window. And thus he remained, wrapped in thought, jotting down an entry now and again in his book, until the train slowed down at Halbury Junction, where we had to change onto a branch line.

As we stepped out I noticed a well-dressed man hurrying up that platform from the rear and eagerly scanning the faces of the few passengers who had alighted. Soon he espied us and, approaching quickly, asked, as he looked from one of us to the other:

"Dr. Thorndyke?"

"Yes," replied my colleague, adding: "And you, I presume, are Mr. Edward Stopford?"

The solicitor bowed. "This is a dreadful affair," he said in an agitated manner. "I see you have the paper. A most shocking affair. I am immensely relieved to find you here. Nearly missed the train, and feared I should miss you."

"There appears to have been an arrest," Thorndyke began.

"Yes—my brother. Terrible business. Let us walk up the platform; our train won't start for a quarter of an hour yet."

We deposited our joint Gladstone and Thorndyke's traveling case in an empty first-class compartment, and then, with the solicitor between us, strolled up to the unfrequented end of the platform.

"My brother's position," said Mr. Stopford, "fills me with dismay—but let me give you the facts in order, and you shall judge for yourself. This poor creature who has been murdered so brutally was a Miss Edith Grant. She was formerly an artist's model, and as such was a good deal employed by my brother, who is a painter—Harold Stopford, you know, A.R.A. now—"

"I know his work very well, and charming work it is."

"I think so too. Well, in those days he was quite a youngster—about twenty—and he became very intimate with Miss Grant, in quite an innocent way, though not very discreet; but she was a nice, respectable girl, as most English models are, and no one thought any harm. However, a good many letters passed between them, and some little presents, amongst which was a beaded chain carrying a locket, and in this he was fool enough to put his portrait and the inscription, 'Edith, from Harold.'

"Later on Miss Grant, who had a rather good voice, went on the stage in the comic-opera line, and in consequence her habits and associates changed somewhat; and, as Harold had meanwhile become engaged, he was naturally anxious to get his letters back, and especially to exchange the locket for some less compromising gift. The letters she eventually sent him, but refused absolutely to part with the locket.

"Now for the last month Harold has been staying at Halbury, making sketching excursions into the surrounding country, and yesterday morning he took the train to Shinglehurst, the third station from here, and the one before Woldhurst.

"On the platform here he met Miss Grant, who had come down from London and was going on to Worthing. They entered the branch train together, having a first-class compartment to themselves. It seems she was wearing his locket at the time, and he made another appeal to her to make an exchange, which she refused, as before.

The discussion appears to have become rather heated and angry on both sides, for the guard and a porter at Munsden both noticed that they seemed to be quarreling; but the upshot of the affair was that the lady snapped the chain and tossed it together with the locket to my brother, and they parted quite amiably at Shinglehurst, where Harold got out. He was then carrying his full sketching kit, including a large holland umbrella, the lower joint of which is an ash staff fitted with a powerful steel spike for driving into the ground.

"It was about half past ten when he got out at Shinglehurst; by eleven he had reached his pitch and got to work, and he painted steadily for three hours. Then he packed up his traps, and was just starting on his way back to the station when he was met by the police and arrested.

"And now, observe the accumulation of circumstantial evidence against him. He was the last person seen in company with the murdered woman —for no one seems to have seen her after they left Munsden; he appeared to be quarreling with her when she was last seen alive, he had a reason for possibly wishing for her death, he was provided with an implement—a spiked staff—capable of inflicting the injury which caused her death, and, when he was searched, there was found in his possession the locket and the broken chain, apparently removed from her person with violence.

"Against all this is, of course, his known character—he is the gentlest and most amiable of men, and his subsequent conduct—imbecile to the last degree if he had been guilty; but, as a lawyer, I can't help seeing that appearances are almost hopelessly against him.''

"We won't say 'hopelessly,'" replied Thorndyke as we took our places in the carriage, "though I expect the police are pretty cocksure. When does the inquest open?"

"Today at four. I have obtained an order from the coroner for you to examine the body and be present at the post-mortem."

"Do you happen to know the exact position of the wound?"

"Yes; it is a little above and behind the left ear—a horrible round hole, with a ragged cut or tear running from it to the side of the forehead."

"And how was the body lying?"

"Right along the floor, with the feet close to the off-side door."

"Was the wound on the head the only one?"

"No; there was a long cut or bruise on the right cheek—a contused wound the police surgeon called it, which he believes to have been inflicted with a heavy and rather blunt weapon. I have not heard of any other wounds or bruises."

"Did anyone enter the train yesterday at Shinglehurst?" Thorndyke asked.

"No one entered the train after it left Halbury."

Thorndyke considered these statements in silence, and presently fell into a brown study, from which he roused only as the train moved out of Shinglehurst station.

"It would be about here that the murder was committed," said Mr. Stopford; "at least, between here and Woldhurst."

Thorndyke nodded rather abstractedly, being engaged at the moment in observing with great attention the objects that were visible from the windows.

"I notice," he remarked presently, "a number of chips scattered about between the rails, and some of the chair wedges look new. Have there been any platelayers at work lately?"

"Yes," answered Stopford, "they are on the line now, I believe—at least, I saw a gang working near Woldhurst yesterday, and they are said to have set a rick on fire; I saw it smoking when I came down."

"Indeed; and this middle line of rails is, I suppose, a sort of siding?"

"Yes, they shunt the goods trains and empty trucks onto it. There are the remains of the rick—still smoldering, you see."

Thorndyke gazed absently at the blackened heap until an empty cattle truck on the middle track hid it from view. This was succeeded by a line of goods wagons, and these by a passenger coach, one compartment of which—a first-class—was closed up and sealed. The train now began to slow down rather suddenly, and a couple of minutes later we brought up in Woldhurst station.

It was evident that rumors of Thorndyke's advent had preceded us, for the entire staff—two porters, an inspector, and the stationmaster—were waiting expectantly on the platform, and the latter came forward, regardless of his dignity, to help us with our luggage.

"Do you think I could see the carriage?" Thorndyke asked the solicitor.

"Not the inside, sir," said the stationmaster, on being appealed to. "The police have sealed it up. You would have to ask the inspector."

"Well, I can have a look at the outside, I suppose?" said Thorndyke.

And to this the stationmaster readily agreed, and offered to accompany us.

"What other first-class passengers were there?" Thorndyke asked.

"None, sir. There was only one first-class coach, and the deceased was the only person in it. It has given us all a dreadful turn, this affair has," he continued as we set off up the line. "I was on the platform when the train came in. We were watching a rick that was burning up the line, and a rare blaze it made, too; and I was just saying that we should have to move the cattle truck that was on the mid track, because you see, sir, the smoke and sparks were blowing across, and I thought it would frighten the poor beasts. And Mr. Felton, he don't like his beasts handled roughly. He says it spoils the meat."

"No doubt he is right," said Thorndyke. "But now, tell me, do you think it is possible for any person to board or leave the train on the off-side unobserved? Could a man, for instance, enter a compartment on the off-side at one station and drop off as the train was slowing down at the next without being seen?"

"I doubt it," replied the stationmaster. "Still, I wouldn't say it is impossible."

"Thank you. Oh, and there's another question. You have a gang of men at work on the line, I see. Now, do those men belong to the district?"

"No, sir; they are strangers, every one, and pretty rough diamonds some of 'em are. But I shouldn't say there was any real harm in 'em. If you was suspecting any of 'em of being mixed up in this—"

"I am not," interrupted Thorndyke rather shortly. "I suspect nobody; but I wish to get all the facts of the case at the outset."

"Naturally, sir," replied the abashed official; and we pursued our way in silence.

"Do you remember, by the way," said Thorndyke as we approached the empty coach, "whether the off-side door of the compartment was closed and locked when the body was discovered?"

"It was closed, sir, but not locked. Why, sir, did you think—"

"Nothing, nothing. The sealed compartment is the one of course?"

Without waiting for a reply he commenced his survey of the coach, while I gently restrained our two companions from shadowing him, as they were disposed to do.

The off-side footboard occupied his attention specially, and when he had scrutinized minutely the part opposite the fatal compartment he walked slowly from end to end with his eyes but a few inches from its surface, as though he was searching for something.

Near what had been the rear end he stopped and drew from his pocket a piece of paper; then with a moistened fingertip he picked up from the footboard some evidently minute object, which he carefully transferred to the paper, folding the latter and placing it in his pocketbook.

He next mounted the footboard and, having peered in through the window of the sealed compartment, produced from his pocket a small insufflator or powder blower, with which he blew a stream of impalpable smokelike powder onto the edges of the middle window, bestowing the closest attention on the irregular dusty patches in which it settled, and even measuring one on the jamb of the window with a pocket rule.

At length he stepped down and, having carefully looked over the near-side footboard, announced that he had finished for the present.

As we were returning down the line we passed a working man who seemed to be viewing the chairs and sleepers with more than casual interest.

"That, I suppose, is one of the platelayers?" Thorndyke suggested to the stationmaster.

"Yes, the foreman of the gang," was the reply.

"I'll just step back and have a word with him, if you will walk on slowly." And my colleague turned back briskly and overtook the man, with whom he remained in conversation for some minutes.

"I think I see the police inspector on the platform," remarked Thorndyke as we approached the station.

"Yes, there he is," said our guide. "Come down to see what you are after, sir, I expect." Which was doubtless the case, although the officer professed to be there by the merest chance.

"You would like to see the weapon, sir, I suppose?" he remarked when he had introduced himself.

"The umbrella spike," Thorndyke corrected. "Yes, if I may. We are going to the mortuary now."

"Then you'll pass the station on the way; so, if you care to look in, I will walk up with you."

This proposition being agreed to, we all proceeded to the police station, including the stationmaster, who was on the very tiptoe of curiosity.

"There you are, sir," said the inspector, unlocking his office and ushering us in. "Don't say we haven't given every facility to the defense. There are all the effects of the accused, including the very weapon the deed was done with."

"Come, come," protested Thorndyke; "we mustn't be premature."

He took the stout ash staff from the officer and, having examined the formidable spike through a lens, drew from his pocket a steel calliper gauge, with which he carefully measured the diameter of the spike and the staff to which it was fixed.

"And now," he said, when he had made a note of the measurements in his book, "we will look at the color box and the sketch. Ha! A very orderly man, your brother, Mr. Stopford. Tubes all in their places, palette knives wiped clean, palette cleaned off and rubbed bright, brushes wiped— they ought to be washed before they stiffen—all this is very significant."

He unstrapped the sketch from the blank canvas to which it was pinned, and, standing it on a chair in a good light, stepped back to look at it.

"And you tell me that that is only three hours' work!" he exclaimed, looking at the lawyer. "It is a really marvelous achievement."

"My brother is a very rapid worker," replied Stopford dejectedly.

"Yes, but this is not only amazingly rapid; it is in his very happiest vein—full of spirit and feeling. But we mustn't stay to look at it longer."

He replaced the canvas on its pins and, having glanced at the locket and some other articles that lay in a drawer, thanked the inspector for his courtesy and withdrew.

"That sketch and the color box appear very suggestive to me," he remarked as we walked up the street.

"To me also," said Stopford gloomily, "for they are under lock and key, like their owner, poor old fellow."

He sighed heavily, and we walked on in silence.

The mortuary keeper had evidently heard of our arrival, for he was waiting at the door with the key in his hand and, on being shown the coroner's order, unlocked the door and we entered together.

But after a momentary glance at the ghostly, shrouded figure lying upon the slate table, Stopford turned pale and retreated, saying that he would wait for us outside with the mortuary keeper.

As soon as the door was closed and locked on the inside, Thorndyke glanced curiously round the bare, whitewashed building.

A stream of sunlight poured in through the skylight and fell upon the silent form that lay so still under its covering sheet, and one stray beam glanced into a corner by the door where, on a row of pegs and a deal table, the dead woman's clothing was displayed.

"There is something unspeakably sad in these poor relics, Jervis," said Thorndyke as we stood before them. "To me they are more tragic, more full of pathetic suggestions, than the corpse itself. See the smart, jaunty hat and the costly skirts hanging there, so desolate and forlorn; the dainty lingerie on the table, neatly folded—by the mortuary man's wife, I hope—the little French shoes and openwork silk stockings. How pathetically eloquent they are of harmless womanly vanity, and the gay, careless life snapped short in the twinkling of an eye. But we must not give way to sentiment. There is another life threatened, and it is in our keeping.''

He lifted the hat from its peg and turned it over in his hand. It was, I think, what is called a "picture hat"—a huge, flat, shapeless mass of gauze and ribbons and feathers, spangled over freely with dark blue sequins. In one part of the brim was a ragged hole, and from this the glittering sequins dropped off in little showers when the hat was moved.

"This will have been worn tilted over on the left side," said Thorndyke, "judging by the general shape and the position of the hole.''

"Yes," I agreed. "Like that of the Duchess of Devonshire in Gainsborough's portrait.''

"Exactly.''

He shook a few of the sequins into the palm of his hand and, replacing the hat on its peg, dropped the little disks into an envelope, on which he wrote, "From the hat," and slipped it into his pocket. Then, stepping over to the table, he drew back the sheet reverently and even tenderly from the dead woman's face and looked down at it with grave pity.

It was a comely face, white as marble, serene and peaceful in expression, with half-closed eyes, and framed with a mass of brassy yellow hair; but its beauty was marred by a long linear wound, half-cut, half-bruise, running down the right cheek from the eye to the chin.

114

"A handsome girl," Thorndyke commented; "a dark-haired blonde. What a sin to have disfigured herself so with that horrible peroxide."

He smoothed the hair back from her forehead and added: "She seems to have applied the stuff last about ten days ago. There is about a quarter of an inch of dark hair at the roots. What do you make of that wound on the cheek?"

"It looks as if she had struck some sharp angle in falling, though, as the seats are padded in first-class carriages, I don't see what she could have struck."

"No. And now let us look at the other wound. Will you note down the description?"

He handed me his notebook, and I wrote down as he dictated:

"A clean-punched circular hole in skull, an inch behind and above margin of left ear—diameter, an inch and seven-sixteenths; starred fracture of parietal bone; membranes perforated and brain entered deeply; ragged scalp wound, extending forward to margin of left orbit; fragments of gauze and sequins in edges of wound. That will do for the present. Dr. Morton will give us further details if we want them."

He pocketed his callipers and rule, drew from the bruised scalp one or two loose hairs, which he placed in the envelope with the sequins, and, having looked over the body for other wounds or bruises (of which there were none) replaced the sheet and prepared to depart.

As we walked away from the mortuary Thorndyke was silent and deeply thoughtful, and I gathered that he was piecing together the facts that he had acquired.

At length Mr. Stopford, who had several times looked at him curiously, said:

"The post-mortem will take place at three, and it is now only half past eleven. What would you like to do next?"

Thorndyke, who in spite of his mental preoccupation had been looking about him in his usual keen, attentive way, halted suddenly.

"Your reference to the post-mortem," said he, "reminds me that I forgot to put the ox gall into my case."

"Ox gall!" I exclaimed, endeavoring vainly to connect this substance with the technique of the pathologist. "What were you going to do with...."

But here I broke off, remembering my friend's dislike of any discussion of his methods before strangers.

"I suppose," he continued, "there would hardly be an artist's color man in a place of this size?"

"I should think not," said Stopford. "But couldn't you get the stuff from a butcher? There's a shop just across the road."

"So there is," agreed Thorndyke, who had already observed the shop. "The gall ought of course to be prepared, but we can filter it ourselves—that is, if the butcher has any. We will try him, at any rate."

He crossed the road towards the shop, over which the name "Felton" appeared in gilt lettering, and, addressing himself to the proprietor, who stood at the door, introduced himself and explained his wants.

"Ox gall?" said the butcher. "No, sir, I haven't any just now; but I am having a beast killed this afternoon, and I can let you have some then. In fact,'' he added, after a pause, ''as the matter is of importance, I can have one killed at once if you wish it.''

''That is very kind of you,'' said Thorndyke, ''and it would greatly oblige me. Is the beast perfectly healthy?''

''They're in splendid condition, sir. I picked them out of the herd myself. But you shall see them—ay, and choose the one that you'd like killed.''

''You are really very good,'' said Thorndyke warmly. ''I will just run into the chemist's next door and get a suitable bottle, and then I will avail myself of your exceedingly kind offer.''

He hurried into the chemist's shop, from which he presently emerged carrying a white paper parcel; and we then followed the butcher down a narrow lane by the side of his shop.

It led to an enclosure containing a small pen, in which were confined three handsome steers, whose glossy black coats contrasted in a very striking manner with their long grayish-white, nearly straight horns.

''These are certainly very fine beasts, Mr. Felton,'' said Thorndyke as we drew up beside the pen, ''and in excellent condition, too.''

He leaned over the pen and examined the beasts critically, especially as to their eyes and horns; then, approaching the nearest one, he raised his stick and bestowed a smart rap on the underside of the right horn, following it by a similar tap on the left one, a proceeding that the beast viewed with stolid surprise.

"The state of the horns," explained Thorndyke as he moved on to the next steer, "enables one to judge to some extent of the beast's health."

"Lord bless you, sir," laughed Mr. Felton, "they haven't got no feeling in their horns, else what good 'ud their horns be to 'em?"

Apparently he was right, for the second steer was as indifferent to a sounding rap on either horn as the first.

Nevertheless, when Thorndyke approached the third steer, I unconsciously drew near to watch; and I noticed that, as the stick struck the horn, the beast drew back in evident alarm, and that then the blow was repeated it became manifestly uneasy.

"He don't seem to like that," said the butcher. "Seems as if—hallo, that's queer!"

Thorndyke had just brought his stick up against the left horn, and immediately the beast had winced and started back, shaking his head and moaning.

There was not, however, room for him to back out of reach, and Thorndyke, by leaning into the pen, was able to inspect the sensitive horn, which he did with the closest attention, while the butcher looked on with obvious perturbation.

"You don't think there's anything wrong with this beast, sir, I hope," said he.

"I can't say without a further examination," replied Thorndyke. "It may be the horn only that is affected. If you will have it sawn off close to the head, and sent up to me at the hotel, I will look at it and tell you. And, by way of preventing any mistakes, I will mark it and cover it up to protect it from injury in the slaughterhouse."

He opened his parcel and produced from it a wide-mouthed bottle labelled "Ox gall," a sheet of gutta-percha tissue, a roller bandage, and a stick of sealing wax.

Handing the bottle to Mr. Felton, he encased the distal half of the horn in a covering by means of the tissue and the bandage, which he fixed securely with the sealing wax.

"I'll saw the horn off and bring it up to the hotel myself, with the ox gall," said Mr. Felton. "You shall have them in half an hour."

He was as good as his word, for in half an hour Thorndyke was seated at a small table by the window of our private sitting room in the Black Bull Hotel.

The table was covered with newspaper, and on it lay the long gray horn and Thorndyke's traveling case, now open and displaying a small microscope and its accessories.

The butcher was seated solidly in an armchair waiting, with a half-suspicious eye on Thorndyke, for the report; and I was endeavoring by cheerful talk to keep Mr. Stopford from sinking into utter despondency, though I too kept a furtive watch on my colleague's rather mysterious proceedings.

I saw him unwind the bandage and apply the horn to his ear, bending it slightly to and fro.

I watched him as he scanned the surface closely through a lens and observed him as he scraped some substance from the pointed end onto a glass slide and, having applied a drop of some reagent, began to tease out the scraping with a pair of mounted needles.

Presently he placed the slide under the microscope and, having observed it attentively for a minute or two, turned round sharply.

"Come and look at this, Jervis," said he.

I wanted no second bidding, being on tenterhooks of curiosity, but came over and applied my eye to the instrument.

"Well, what is it?" he asked.

"A multipolar nerve corpuscle—very shriveled, but unmistakable."

"And this?"

He moved the slide to a fresh spot.

"Two pyramidal nerve corpuscles and some portions of fibers."

"And what do you say the tissue is?"

"Cortical brain substance, I should say, without a doubt."

"I entirely agree with you. And that being so," he added, turning to Mr. Stopford, "we may say that the case for the defense is practically complete."

"What in heaven's name do you mean?" exclaimed Stopford, starting up.

"I mean that we can now prove when and where and how Miss Grant met her death. Come and sit down here, and I will explain. No, you needn't go away, Mr. Felton. We shall have to subpoena you. Perhaps," he continued, "we had better go over the facts and see what they suggest. And first we note the position of the body, lying with the feet close to the off-side door, showing that, when she fell, the deceased was sitting, or more probably standing, close to that door. Next there is this."

He drew from his pocket a folded paper, which he opened, displaying a tiny blue disk.

"It is one of the sequins with which her hat was trimmed, and I have in this envelope several more which I took from the hat itself.

"This single sequin I picked up on the rear end of the off-side footboard, and its presence there makes it nearly certain that at some time Miss Grant had put her head out of the window on that side.

"The next item of evidence I obtained by dusting the margins of the off-side window with a light powder, which made visible a greasy impression three-and-a-quarter inches long on the sharp corner of the right-hand jamb (right-hand from the inside, I mean).

"And now as to the evidence furnished by the body. The wound in the skull is behind and above the left ear, is roughly circular, and measures one inch and seven-sixteenths at most, and a ragged scalp wound runs from it towards the left eye. On the right cheek is a linear contused wound three-and-a-quarter inches long. There are no other injuries.

"Our next facts are furnished by this."

He took up the horn and tapped it with his fingers, while the solicitor and Mr. Felton stared at him in speechless wonder.

"You notice it is a left horn, and you remember that it was highly sensitive. If you put your ear to it while I strain it, you will hear the grating of a fracture in the bony core.

"Now look at the pointed end, and you will see several deep scratches running lengthwise, and where those scratches end the diameter of the horn is, as you see by this calliper gauge, one inch and seven-sixteenths. Covering the scratches is a dry bloodstain, and at the extreme tip is a small mass of a dried substance which Dr. Jervis and I have examined with the microscope and are satisfied is brain tissue."

"Good God!" exclaimed Stopford eagerly. "Do you mean to say—"

"Let us finish with the facts, Mr. Stopford," Thorndyke interrupted. "Now, if you look closely at that bloodstain, you will see a short piece of hair stuck to the horn, and through this lens you can make out the root bulb. It is a golden hair, you notice, but near the root it is black, and our calliper gauge shows us that the black portion is fourteen sixty-fourths of an inch long.

"Now in this envelope are some hairs that I removed from the dead woman's head. They also are golden hairs, black at the roots, and when I measure the black portion I find it to be fourteen sixty-fourths of an inch long. Then, finally, there is this."

He turned the horn over and pointed to a small patch of dried blood. Embedded in it was a blue sequin.

Mr. Stopford and the butcher gazed at the horn in silent amazement; then the former drew a deep breath and looked up at Thorndyke.

"No doubt," said he, "you can explain this mystery, but for my part I am utterly bewildered, though you are filling me with hope."

"And yet the matter is quite simple," returned Thorndyke, "even with these few facts before us, which are only a selection from the body of evidence in our possession. But I will state my theory, and you shall judge."

He rapidly sketched a rough plan on a sheet of paper and continued:

"These were the conditions when the train was approaching Woldhurst. Here was the passenger coach, here was the burning rick, and here was a cattle truck. This steer was in that truck. Now my hypothesis is that at that time Miss Grant was standing with her head out of the off-side window, watching the burning rick. Her wide hat, worn on the left side, hid from her view the cattle truck which she was approaching, and then this is what happened."

He sketched another plan to a larger scale.

"One of the steers—this one—had thrust its long horn out through the bars. The point of that horn struck the deceased's head, driving her face violently against the corner of the window, and then, in disengaging, ploughed its way through the scalp and suffered a fracture of its core from the violence of the wrench. This hypothesis is inherently probable, it fits all the facts, and those facts admit of no other explanation."

The solicitor sat for a moment as though dazed; then he rose impulsively and seized Thorndyke's hands.

"I don't know what to say to you," he exclaimed huskily, "except that you have saved my brother's life, and for that may God reward you!"

The butcher rose from his chair with a slow grin.

"It seems to me," said he, "as if that ox gall was what you might call a blind, eh, sir?"

And Thorndyke smiled an inscrutable smile.

When we returned to town on the following day we were a party of four, which included Mr. Harold Stopford.

The verdict of "Death by misadventure," promptly returned by the coroner's jury, had been shortly followed by his release from custody, and he now sat with his brother and me, listening with rapt attention to Thorndyke's analysis of the case.

"So you see," the latter concluded, "I had six possible theories of the cause of death worked out before I reached Halbury, and it only remained to select the one that fitted the facts. And when I had seen the cattle truck, had picked up that sequin, had heard the description of the steers, and had seen the hat and the wounds, there was nothing left to do but the filling in of details."

"And you never doubted my innocence?" asked Harold Stopford.

Thorndyke smiled at his quondam client.

"Not after I had seen your color box and your sketch," said he; "to say nothing of the spike."